MAKING
MEMORY

MAKING MEMORY

V C Sanford

CHAPTER 1

IN THE BEGINNING...

The ragged screech of the cherry red airbrakes as the overloaded yellow school bus slowed to a stop snapped me from my daydream; startling me out of Topper's muscular embrace and back to the dismal reality that was my life. I jumped up from the seat, bumping into a senior jock that was walking down the aisle and dropped my book bag onto the foot of the snooty cheerleader I had been stuck sitting next to.

"Stupid bitch. Go sit with the rest of the losers in the front of the bus."

My initial thought was to tell her exactly where she could go. It was times like this I wished I had the guts to say what was on my mind. Instead, I snatched the bag up with a stammered apology and dashed for the exit before the asshole driver decided to pull away from my stop. At least twice a week I was forced to ride three extra blocks to the next stop and then walk back along the heavily traveled bi-pass to reach my own street. Luckily, one of the younger kids had her hands full offloading a bulky school project. It made a longer stop necessary, giving me the extra time to reach the door before the fat fool pulled away.

In seven weeks I would be sixteen; old enough to drive and get a real job. It would also allow me to document my ability to support myself, making me eligible to apply for emancipated minor status under state law. I can't wait to be free of the system. Of course, being old enough didn't guarantee anything except the eligibility. First, I had to pass the driver's license test, and then I had to somehow convince Mrs. Tolbert, my foster mother, that I was responsible enough to work part-time after school. Between babysitting and odd jobs I'd managed to pick up around the neighborhood, I'd managed to save a little over a thousand dollars, not enough for a good car, but enough for a hoop-dee crap car that was little more than a piece of junk.

I blinked back a tear, remembering how my father had worked alongside my brother in the garage as they painstakingly restored Bobby's old Ford pickup. I would not have his help, but I had watched and remembered most of the lessons he had taught Bobby about restoring older cars.

It would not be easy, but I could do it. My afterschool job would cover insurance, gas, and repairs. As long as I saved my money and did not splurge too often on luxuries, I could handle it. Experience had shown me how quickly my carefully laid plans could go to hell in a handbasket, but after the last four years, I figured I didn't have anything left to lose.

I stopped and grabbed the mail from the box before following the other kids down the gravel drive to the rambling yellow house I now called home. It was pleasant enough place to live, although a little crowded with six other foster kids living there. Mrs. Tolbert always made sure there was plenty of good, nourishing food to eat, even though it was usually the cheaper cuts of chicken and lots of hamburger helper. She cooked it all from scratch, making sure we had fresh vegetables and fruit with each meal, and even provided the occasional special treat. The food alone made it a thousand times better than any other foster home I had lived in.

As the oldest, I even had a room to myself. It was small, little more than an oversized closet with a window, but it was large enough for my twin bed and the small chest of drawers that held my clothes. Best of all, it had a door that I could close, giving me a small sense of privacy. Mrs. Tolbert had allowed me to paint it baby blue with lime green trim, my two favorite colors. She even bought me sheets and a bedspread to match. I had made a simple bulletin board and hung it above the bed after decorating it with pictures I had cut from magazines and a few of my better papers from school.

It had taken me a while to overcome my trust issues, but considering everything I'd been through since the accident, that could be expected. Despite my initial reservations, it was starting to feel like home.

There was a strange car in the driveway, a sedan similar to the ones usually driven by the social workers from the Department of Family and Children Services. Normally, the sight of the sedan would have caused my stomach to tighten into a knot, but things had been good since I'd had been placed with Mrs. Tolbert. After being in six different foster homes over the last four years, I had finally found a place I could be happy.

No, today the worker had to be there about

one of the others. Perhaps the twins, Tyrel and Tyrese? I'd had overheard Mrs. Tolbert discussing the possibility of them returning to their mother's care with her friend Regina just last night. They would be so happy, they missed their mother and talked about her all the time.

Sure enough, the lady in the living room had a stack of papers with her and Mrs. Tolbert was busy signing them one by one. She had been crying and had a small pile of used tissue lying just to the right of the paper stack. Mrs. Tolbert always cried when one of her children left, even when they were being returned to their parents. She was just that kind of person.

Still, it had to be good news, or she wouldn't be smiling while she cried. I pasted a smile on my face and made an effort to be polite, figuring it would reflect well in the lady's report on the foster home. If the twins went home, that left two open beds, and the possibility of them placing a girl my age increased.

I was humming the latest Drake song under my breath as I dropped the mail into the basket on the counter, picked up a cookie from the plate nearby and poured myself a glass of milk. I turned away from the refrigerator, then froze; a heavy lump growing in the pit of my stomach as my heart began pounding in my chest. Mrs. Tolbert and the DFACS lady were standing just inside the kitchen doorway and both of them were looking straight at me.

Oh, no. It can't be happening again.

Then everything went black.

***

I was stretched out on the sofa in the living room when I awakened, and Mrs. Tolbert had my head in her lap. She had been crying again, I could still make out the faint, glistening trail of her tears on her makeup. My heart was still pounding in my chest and I was having difficulty drawing a complete breath, so it came out in short panting gasps.

The social worker was staring at me like I was some type of illegal alien, that had fainted just to add a massive delay into her already overly full schedule. I wondered if that if I pretended to be ill, they might leave me where I was. It was a distinct possibility.

Before I could decide on the perfect amount of drama needed to convince her to leave me where I was, she stood and picked up her things.

"Have her ready to go at eight a.m. The court

appointed escort will be here to pick her up, and they have to be at the station by nine. Don't bother getting up, you have your hands full. I can show myself out."

She left before I had a chance to show her my imminent death scene, which sucked because I was really beginning to feel sick.

At least Mrs. Tolbert seemed to understand what I was feeling. She pulled me into her arms; smoothing back my long dark hair, tucking a few strands behind my ear, then planted a big kiss on my forehead.

"I'm going to miss you," she whispered. She held me as I cried myself to sleep, leaving me on the sofa alone in the darkness when she finally slipped off to get the others ready for bed.

CHAPTER 2

CHA...CHA...CHA...CHANGES

At approximately two o'clock I glanced at my wristwatch for the hundredth time and began staring out the train windows for the first sign of a metropolitan city. So far, all I could see was farmland and mountains covered with lots of trees. The tracks followed the terrain and other than the old steel girder bridge we had just crossed, there was nothing much to break up the monotony.

At least there seemed to be a variety of trees here. Not the skinny palms and decorative Japanese maples everyone planted back home. These were ancient oaks and pine forests, on hillsides too heavily overgrown for development. I was looking forward to exploring once I reached my destination.

The train was scheduled to arrive in Nashville at two fifteen but the baggage handler at the station had laughingly told me it was never on time.

"It's a southern thing to be fashionably late," he said as he loaded my battered suitcase into the overhead rack when we transferred from one train to another in Cincinnati.

"Nobody's in a hurry; whatever it is you need to do, it will still be waiting when you get there." He winked. "That's why women up north look older than our southern belles. They are always frowning about something not getting done. Gives 'em lines between the eyebrows and tiny ones around the corners of their mouth. Take it from me, you just be thankful you are going to be living in the south and not the north."

I had tried my best to relax as he said it, but the nervous tension I felt throughout my body would not give me a break. So much had happened in so short a time, my system was overloaded.

Ms. Logan, the DFACS lady who came with the escort the next morning, had explained the situation the best way she could, considering the limited information she had been provided.

"Someone has come forward with documentation proving they are relatives of yours. They have petitioned the court for guardianship and have been granted all legal rights and full custody. The Winter's, your aunt and uncle, want you to come and live with them and their daughter Hannah. She's the same age as you."

I mumbled something about *big toothy inbred cultists,* and she ignored me.

"After thinking you have no living relatives, it has to feel unreal. Since you have been part of the system for almost a third of your life, it will be a big change. I understand from the paperwork that they live on a small farm in the Northern part of Georgia, but I have no idea what they raise. It could be cattle or some plant foods. Farm life can be fun, despite all the stories about getting up at dawn to do chores. After living in Los Angeles, it will take a little while for you to adjust to the rural lifestyle. The court feels it will be a great opportunity for you to start over, and I agree."

Gee, so much better. Just change cultist to hayseeds.

I sat on the edge of the sofa and pressed my lips tightly together to keep from telling her exactly how little I cared about her opinion, or the courts ideas about what would be good for me. My life had finally arrived at a good place and once again, they were tearing me away from the tiny bit of happiness I'd managed to scrape together. I wanted to run away. Go anywhere except to Georgia. Even the name sounded hick. And the case worker kept going on and on about how perfect they were.

"If they are that perfect, why did they wait six years to come and find me?"

"They obviously went to a lot of trouble to locate you. We had no idea that you had any living relatives at all, much less an entire family of cousins and their children."

Cousins. There was more of them? My parents hadn't spoken much about their life in Georgia. I always figured it must have been pretty sad, for them to run clear across the country to get away from their families. Bobby might have had a better idea of what was going on, but he never spoke about anything unless he had too. My brother had been big on keeping secrets.

I could picture it all in my mind, my dad growing up on the reservation and my mother working on the family farm. I could see them now, meeting at the goodwill in town, talking while their mothers shopped for decent second-hand clothes. I bet they both rode for an hour each morning before daylight to get to school on a rural school bus. No wonder the two of them had run away.

I had already been withdrawn from school by Ms. Logan and the transfer papers were inside the large manila envelope I'd placed in my suitcase. That hadn't really bothered me, I didn't have any real friends at school anyway. But it would have been nice to be asked if I had anyone to tell goodbye.

At home, Mrs. Tolbert had watched as I packed my clothing in the same ratty old suitcase. I had been using it for the last six years. As I dropped the neatly folded stacks inside, I noticed that one of my tee shirts and a pair of ankle boots were missing from my closet. I had a good idea who had taken them, but it wasn't worth fighting over. I doubted there would be anywhere in the mountains to wear the white swede boots anyway. They wouldn't last long while mucking out stalls or chasing chickens around a pen. I wondered what they produced on the farm anyway. With my luck, it would turn out to be a pig farm.

As I walked down the hallway to the living room where the strange women waited, I did my best to control the emotions that fought to escape my wavering restraints. The other children were quiet for once; it felt almost as if they would really miss me after I was gone.

Except for Kayleigh; she was next oldest and would inherit my room after I was gone. She had spent the last hour babbling about how she was going to redecorate her new room. I imagined my cheerful room covered in Goth blacks and greys, with a hint of mauve or purple. It made me shudder.

Mrs. Tolbert tried not to cry but I could still see the tears welling in her eyes. She was still in the yard waving bye as the dark grey sedan turned the corner and I lost sight of the house.

***

At the train station, I was placed into the care of an elderly woman who made her living accompanying wards of the state whenever they needed to travel. She was a stout lady in her middle fifties, with closely cropped steel grey hair and horn-rimmed glasses that only emphasized the quiet determination of her mouth. Her icy blue eyes flashed when she talked, reinforcing her manner of crisp authority. I immediately thought *arrogant old witch*. There were a few other words I could use to describe her, but I somehow refrained from expressing them out loud. The trip across the country was going to be long enough without irritating the old biddy any more than necessary.

"My name is Ms. Marsh, and I expect to be addressed in that way. You may also say yes or no Ma'am."

At that comment, I let a snort of laughter slip through my pursed lips, thinking she was the epidemy of a '*middle-aged molester*.' I knew there was no way I could say Ma'am without breaking into laughter, so I made a decision to say as little as possible during the train trip. It wasn't like she was going to be an important part of my life anyway.

The sudden eyebrow arch and glare she gave me, left me feeling cold. She looked me up and down, taking in the ruddy bronze skin I'd inherited from my Cherokee father and the shamrock green eyes my mother had gifted me with. I was certain she thought I was Latino. Simply another of the anchor kids dumped by the coyotes after using them to get across the border. Here next words confirmed my guess.

"At least you understand English, my Spanish is weak. I have a few rules I expect you to follow while you are in my care. The first is 'Please refrain from talking unless I address you first.'"

She waited until I nodded, and then continued.

"You must understand, I am very familiar with teenage girls and their habits. I do not want to be disturbed unless an emergency occurs, and then, only if there is no other alternative. You are to read or watch television while the train is in motion--,"

She took a sip from her teacup.

"--allowing me time to catch up on my rest. If I am reading or knitting, you will not talk to me or make excessive noise, nor are you to wander around the railway cars bothering the other passengers. If you are hungry, you are allowed to go to the dining car for a snack but only if you cannot wait until after my nap." She pulled her knitting bag closer to her seat and took out two shiny brass needles and a skein of pale blue yarn.

When she began to knit, I got the hint; she was not expecting me to answer her. I settled down in the seat opposite to the one she as in and stared out the window at the passing scenery. We had a small private sleeper compartment with narrow bunk style beds above the bench chairs. All of the cross country train travel would take a couple of days to complete, so we needed the sleeper car at least until we arrived in Chicago.

Apparently, we would travel from Las Angeles to Chicago, a little over 2200 miles. That would take forty-three hours and eat up two days. In Chicago, we would change trains going southeast to Cincinnati, another nine-hour ride and then change again going south to Nashville on the City of New Orleans, a rather famous train that a song was written about. That would eat up another ten hours. In Nashville, we were to take a shuttle service that runs to Chattanooga but that was only three hours, so it was not so bad. So if nothing went wrong, in less than four days we would be meeting my relatives in Chattanooga for the transfer. Once I was safely ensconced in my new relatives' custody, she would reverse the trip and go back to L.A. It was one hell of a cray-cray way to make a living.

It only took about half an hour after leaving the station before the repetitive motion of the train lulled my soon to be erstwhile guardian into a deep sleep. It made me wonder what she'd been sipping from when I was not in the room. I considered ways to escape the moving train but realized that would be a stupid move. My suitcase held everything I owned and the money I had saved would not last long on the street. It would be better to wait until the transfer of custody was complete and then take off from Georgia. That way I would not be escaping government custody and they would have to give me at least forty-eight hours to put some distance between us before I could be declared missing. I sat and watched the old woman sleep a few minutes, listening to the rumbling snores grow slower and deeper; then I decided to explore my new environment.

The train was a long one with two engines and twenty cars. Seven of the twenty carried passengers. Most of the passenger cars were filled with rows of seats, two on each side of the aisle that reclined slightly to allow some limited form of sleep. Two of them were sleeper cars like the one we were staying in, filled with tiny compartments containing bunks and couches that let down into beds for sleeping. The sleepers were designed for people traveling long distances such as the trip we were making from California to Georgia. It would take three days to go coast to coast and I was already dreading the time I had to spend with the horrible Ms. March.

One wonderful discovery was the reading room. It was stocked with many of the larger metropolitan newspapers as well as two computer stations set up for web surfing. Since the time had to be shared there was a signup sheet on which I could schedule time for my own usage. There were already two teenage boys busy at the computer stations and two others were waiting for their chance.

One of the boys, a skinny redhead covered in freckles looked me up and down with a cocky leer, then rolled his eyes at something the other boy said. He stretched, and snatched the baseball cap from his head, allowing a mass of greasy, dark locks to fall around his shoulders, then laughed when the dark-haired boy knocked his drink over trying to get it back.

Neither were worth my time, so I ignored their antics and asked the attendant where the list was. After studying the signup sheet, I decided to request time later in the evening after many of the younger kids would be asleep. It would also give me an excuse to leave Ms. March to her tedious soap operas. If I worked it right, I would finish my time with the computers right before my normal bedtime. Plus, since many of the passengers had brought their own laptop and were taking advantage of the free wireless, the possibility of meeting a few people nearer my age improved after the young ones went to bed. A quick shower and straight into bed and I could pretty much avoid the wizened old dragon completely. Then repeat for the next four days.

The soft rumbling of my stomach reminded me that I had started out with the intention of locating the dining car. I suddenly found myself ravenously hungry.

My first-class ticket included meals, so I did not have to worry about money. My savings were safe, hidden inside the lining of my old suitcase. No one would ever expect to find anything of value in that ratty old case. Thinking of my savings reminded me of my now useless emancipation plans. Once again, I was looking forward to spending another birthday celebration without friends. But at least I had my new family to look forward to. *Yeah, right...*

Family? They were a bunch of strangers sharing my DNA, or at least that's what I'd been told. I knew absolutely nothing about them other than what was on my custody papers. Their last name was Winters, not Cruz. I had been told that my maternal grandmother was also theirs. I wondered how they had found me, in a foster home all the way across the country. An even more important question was why had they bothered?

CHAPTER 3

TRAIN

The last hour of the cross-country train trip was one of the longest hours I could remember. Not that it wasn't interesting. The train was traveling through the Piedmont section of Tennessee, passing thru, around and over mountainous terrain that looked completely different from the ocean side area I had grown up in. The late spring weather was co-operating for a change and instead of heavy rain, we were treated to balmy sunshine. It was almost as warm as it had been back home.

Even though I had enjoyed the train trip, I was excited when the conductor announced the Nashville stop. Soon I would meet my mysterious cousins and travel with them to my new home, not that I was excited about living on a country farm. Since Nashville was the nearest city to their North Georgia home that Amtrak serviced, Mr. Winters had arranged for us to travel by shuttle from Nashville to Chattanooga. He was going to meet us at the old train terminal downtown. My court-ordered shadow had called from Nashville when we boarded the shuttle, and they knew the approximate time that we would arrive.

JaMicah; the friendly bellman on the City of New Orleans had spent a little of his time talking with me the day before we arrived in Nashville. He talked about the historic train, offering a bit of trivia and then mentioned he was born and raised in Chattanooga. You could tell he was proud of his hometown. He even gave me some background on the old station.

"Chattanooga's Terminal Station was built in 1909 and served as the heart of bustling railway activity until trains were replaced by alternate modes of transportation. The last train stopped on August 11, 1970. The station was formerly named the Union Station because several different Rail Road lines ended there. During the Civil War, it was used as a hospital by both armies. During World War II Glen Miller and his orchestra recorded a song by Harry Warren and Mack Gordon. That song; The Chattanooga Choo-Choo, made track 29 famous. It became an instant success, remaining on the pop charts for seventeen weeks in 1941, and is still played by Golden Oldie stations today."

JaMicah smiled, showing me some of the straightest, whitest teeth I'd ever seen. I wondered if the were real, they were so perfect. My teeth were okay, but they were more ivory than white, and it was a constant battle to keep the cavities under control.

"If you are remaining in the Chattanooga area, you should visit the Trolley Barn and the Chattanooga Rail Road Museum. You can see where I grew up from the museum parking lot."

Micah made it sound fascinating and I hoped that my new relatives would allow me a chance to explore before rushing me out to the country.

Ms. March seemed eager to see me on my way, urging me to gather my belongings and be ready to exit the shuttle immediately after it arrived in Chattanooga. We would have to take a taxi from the shuttle station at the local airport and then to the Chattanooga Choo Choo Hotel downtown, where we were meeting my new family.

"Do you have everything?" She repeated this more than once, in between leaning back and forth across the small shuttle bus and staring out the window at the increasing traffic.

I wondered if her pay was predicated on my safe delivery? It was almost worth disappearing just to see her panicked reaction. With my luck, she'd have a heart attack and die, and I'd be haunted by that the rest of my life. If I didn't get blamed for it and spend the rest of my life in jail.

Despite my inner demon prompting me to enact my own version of Karma, I managed to stay seated, spending the last few moments of the trip trying to visualize what my new cousins would look like. I knew that they were in their mid-forties, with one daughter, Hannah who was a few months older than I was. Mattias Winters, the father, and my second or third cousin was a computer programmer. He worked at home, doing subcontract work for the Federal Government. Peggy was his wife and she volunteered at Murray County High School but did not work. Supposedly they were comfortably well off and did not need the money. Hannah was their only child.

I tried to picture them in my mind, but I had too little info to build an image from. I was medium height and slender, with waist length dark auburn brown hair. I was always told I looked a lot like my father, who was a full-blooded Cherokee, but I had a lot of my mother in me too. I vaguely remembered hearing Margot, my mother, discussing how they had met in high school. They had run off together because her family did not approve of their relationship. After hearing all the comments made about southern rednecks on the news, I could only imagine how difficult it must have been.

Billy Hornbuckle, my father, was born on the Cherokee Reservation near the Qualla Boundary; in the area they called Big Cove. His family chose to leave the reservation, moving to Murray County, Georgia near the Tennessee State line. Billy's father was a mechanic who ran a small garage in Copperhill, supporting Billy and his five brothers without aid from the government. I was certain that I had cousins from his side of the family in the area somewhere but did not expect to ever meet any of them.

Daddy had taken the last name Cruz in California since everyone thought he was Mexican anyway. I always thought that hilarious since not one of us spoke Spanish. It had its downside too. Supposedly, it was that name change that had made it so difficult for my relatives to be located…or to locate me. Cruz was about as common as Smith or Jones in Latino areas, kinda like Hernandez and Rodriguez.

Even after six years I still remembered my mother as a beautiful, soft-spoken woman who never raised her voice and was always smiling. She was about the same height and weight as me but that was where the similarity ended. My mother had creamy white skin and long, wavy, silvery blonde hair. Where I had trouble with basic dance steps, my mother danced like a ballerina, seeming to float gracefully around, while somehow making it seem natural. I couldn't even pull off the 'Dougie' without everyone laughing.

My mother's voice had been clear and bright, almost musical when she talked. She had loved to sing to me; usually old mountain folk songs that her mother had sung to her as a child. I hadn't thought a lot about that until we reached the foothills of the Appalachians and it started to sink in that I was going to be living near her home. I would be able to see with my own eyes the places she'd described to me before she died.

The one thing I did inherit from my mother was her eyes. They were unique, almond shaped with long dark lashes framing eyes of the most amazing violet blue. Unique at least until I looked out the window of the taxi as it rolled to a stop in front of the station. There, standing with a tall blonde haired man, was a slender silvery-haired woman staring back at me with the exact same color eyes.

CHAPTER 4

MEET THE FAMILY

Most of my two-hour trip to Winter's Cove from the hotel in Chattanooga was spent in a vacuous daze listening to Mattias and Peggy talk about my mother's childhood and my new home. By asking a few pointed questions I was able to learn the answers to a lot of questions that had haunted me throughout my childhood. But it didn't take long for me to realize they were not going to give out information freely. It wasn't that they were rude, it was more that they were extremely careful in what they said. I made me wonder what they were hiding.

Peggy was forty-three, only a year older than my mother would be if she had lived. She had grown up about a half mile away from my mother's family farm in Winters Cove. The two had been close friends throughout childhood and it was a letter my mother had mailed her just before the accident that had led them to find me.

Peggy showed me an old picture of my parents, my brother and myself taken on the beach near Malibu. I had been about 9 at the time, so it must have a little less than a year before they had died. It wasn't easy to keep my emotions under control, I had never seen the photo before, and it was the only one I'd ever seen with all four of us in it. My eyes welled up with unshed tears. Not wanting to ask for a Kleenex, I used the back of my sleeve to wipe them away, knowing how many times my mother had chewed me for doing exactly that.

"When we get home, I will make you a copy to keep. If we blow it up, you can frame it for your room."

I had nodded in response, the tightness in my throat making it difficult to speak. Peggy seemed to understand because she changed the conversation to Winter's Cove, my new home.

"I think you will like living here. Winter's Cove is a private valley located deep within the foothills of the Appalachian Mountains near the Cohutta Wilderness Preserve. The only way to reach the valley is a gated private road off of Old Highway 2."

Great, not only are they all hillbillies, they

are privacy nuts too. She didn't seem to notice how little I cared, I wasn't going to be around for long. Definitely not long enough to explore the neighborhood.

"There were about twenty families living in the valley. Most of them work from home or in the nearby city of McCaysville. Like your mother, everyone is related to Jero Winters or at least to one of his descendants since Jero died during World War II."

That caught my attention. Everyone in the valley was related to my mother?

"You will be going to Murray County High. We homeschool the kids when they are young, but most choose the public school experience when they are old enough to go, though I have no idea why."

Me either. I hated going to public school.

"Hannah goes to Murray High," Mattias said with a wry grin. "She usually drives herself, even though she's not supposed to drive without an adult in the car. There is a private bus that picks up at each house."

That was interesting. A bus that picked up just my cousins? Wonder what they did that necessitated being separated from the other kids.

"When will I meet Hannah?"

Mattias and Peggy looked at each other for a moment before Peggy answered.

"Hannah is at a memorial today. One of your cousins, Michael Winters passed away last week. The funeral was yesterday but the younger folk in the valley wanted to have their own memory service. It may be late before she gets home. Since today is Saturday, it might be sometime tomorrow before you get a chance to meet her."

Hmmm, was that because Hannah stayed out all night partying or because she slept late? Her mother didn't appear too upset about her absence. After six years of ten o'clock curfews, it would be great to stay out later without getting grounded.

"Monday I will drive you into town and register you for school. For now, it will be enough to get settled into your room."

We turned off the winding state highway onto a short deceleration lane before stopping at an elaborate wrought iron gate complete with a uniformed security guard and a large German Shepherd.

"George, my uncle said as he called the older guard over, this is my cousin Memory. I want you to get a good look and make sure you will recognize her. I'm sure you won't have any trouble remembering her name."

I winced as he did the same thing so many others had done, making the sad joke about remembering my name.

"No sir, Mr. Winters, I don't think I will have any trouble remembering her." He looked at me and winked and I suddenly realized he was at least half Cherokee himself. The short grey hair had thrown me off at first, but once my mind put it together, it was obvious he was Native American too.

I was surprised to find that once we passed through the arched stone entrance, all the roads within the valley were paved and well maintained. After a twenty minute drive along the access road, we passed a second set of gates and entered into Winters Cove itself.

Driving through the exclusive neighborhood of manicured lawns and Georgian Mansions, I realized I might have been a bit off with my mental images of my mother's childhood. This was more Beverly Hillbillies than Lil Abner. Every building we passed would have been at home in the Hollywood Hills. The closest we came to a farm, was an enormous arena and several fields of grazing beef cattle inside white clapboard fence.

Mattias and Peggy took the second right, a winding lane that gradually climbed about half-way up the ridge. Their home was beautiful, a two-story glass and log cabin whose architecture blended into the side of the mountain. A plump Cocker Spaniel and an excited German Sheppard greeted then, circling the car and barking exuberantly until an older woman in a flour-covered apron shooed them away.

"Welcome Home! She called down from the doorway. "I did not think you would ever get here. Come here girl and let me get a good look at you."

"Don't mind Mama," Mattias said jovially. "She sometimes forgets that not everyone is an instant friend. It must be a southern thing because all of my relatives are the same way. First, she will examine you, then she will feed you, you wait and see."

Sure enough, it was not long before I found myself settled comfortably into an oversized leather recliner, a glass of coke in one hand and a slice of German Chocolate cake in the other.

"Once you finish your snack, I will show you to your room. I hope you like it. Mama Dodi and I spent all last week getting it ready."

Memory smiled. "I am sure it will be wonderful. I hate that I am putting you to such trouble."

"No trouble! No trouble at all," Peggy answered. "We are your family and you are more than welcome. I realize it's been hard for you to assimilate all the changes that have happened to your life in such a short time. Don't try to absorb it all, just understand we really do want you here."

"Well," a soft female voice whispered; "at least some of us do."

Startled, I looked around but there was no one in the room except Peggy. I shrugged, deciding it must have been my imagination. But in the back of my mind, I wondered if something might be wrong with me. Maybe it was a residual effect of the accident and I was just now noticing it.

Peggy and Mattias both looked guilty, like a child caught with his hand in the cookie jar. And even though they were behaving as if they had not heard anything, I felt that they both had, but was covering it up for some reason.

"I know you are tired after your long trip. Perhaps you would like to go to your room now and get settled in. Mattias will bring up your bag in a moment." Peggy motioned for me to precede her up the stairs, and then led the way once we reached the landing.

My new room was the last door on the left, near the back side of the house. I figured it had been a guest room at one time because I could smell the new paint scent even though they had used a really nice floral coverup. Taking a deep breath, I stopped in the doorway and took it all in. It was like something out of a magazine. Chiefly decorated in pale shades of blue and lime green, the room included everything any teenage girl could ever imagine, or want, in a bedroom. An enormous sleigh bed dominated the room; piled high with comforters and lacy pillows. Next to the bed sat two matching end tables topped with etched glass. There was a comfortable chaise lounge sitting by the bay window, offering me a perfect place to curl up a good book. A small bookcase nearby held a selection of the latest popular teen books for me to choose from. Two doors led off the room; one to an enormous walk-in closet that I could never imagine filling, the other into a tastefully decorated private bath. I stood in the doorway staring, certain I had just died and gone to heaven.

***

Mattias laid her suitcase on the bed and tried not to show his dismay over how light it was. The poor girls' entire life was inside a suitcase barely big enough to hold Hannah's make up, much less a weeks' worth of clothing.

He made a mental note to discuss with Peggy the possibility of a shopping expedition to the small clothing store in McCaysville tomorrow. The store did not have a large variety, but it did carry a lot of staples, something it seemed Memory desperately needed. The shoes she was wearing looked like they came from the dollar store and the rest of her clothing were clearly hand me downs. Teenagers could be rough on a newcomer and the kids in Winter's Cove were terrors to anyone they felt did not belong within their circle.

Perhaps Hannah? No, that was not going to happen. Hannah had made her feelings clear. Poor girl, living in the valley was difficult enough when you had parents. Without buffers, Memory was going to be in for a rough time. The next two months could be the last two of her life, and she had no idea what was coming. He pulled the door shut behind him.

*****

Mattias poured himself a cup of coffee and then joined his wife and his mother at the kitchen table.

"How about a piece of pie with that?" Peggy offered. "Dodi made it today. It's peach, your favorite."

"Sounds good to me, got any ice cream left?"

"Nope, Hannah ate the last of it, last night. She claims she was drowning her sorrow over Michael's death, but I think she was just angry over Memory's arrival."

"Hannah should understand by now why it is so important for Memory to be here. There is not much time left as it is. Memory's a smart girl, I can see that already. I wonder how much she suspects?"

"Considering how abnormal her life has been up to this point unless we come right out and tell her, she may never suspect, at least until it is too late to do anything about it. I swear she heard your Mama's comments."

"For now, just keep an eye on her. We still have time, so let's wait and see what happens before making any definite decision. One wrong move at this time and she could end up like Michael. And we've buried enough this year."

CHAPTER 5

FIRST DAY AT NEW SCHOOL

The final bell rang at precisely three P.M. and for me, it was the prettiest sound I had heard all day. Not that the first day at Murray High was any different than the first day at any of the other eight schools I had attended since my parent's accident. It was creepy. All day long I could sense everyone watching my every move. My skin was literally crawling. It was all I could do not to run out the door as soon as the teacher dismissed us for the day.

It had begun early, almost as soon as I had entered the front door of the amazedly clean school. The walls were freshly painted, and I would bet my life's savings it wasn't to cover up graffiti someone had painted on the walls when the teacher wasn't looking.

I had never seen an administration staff so polite and attentive. When they walked into the office, Peggy was addressed by name. We were taken immediately back into the councilors office and my registration was completed in minutes. They already had my transcripts and new class schedule printed up.

When the bell rang for my first-period class the counselor, Mr. Dickenson, actually walked me to class. If that wasn't strange enough, he introduced me to my homeroom teacher, Mr. Stone as Memory Winters, not Cruz.

"Excuse me, but my name is Memory Cruz, not Winters. I usually go by Memory."

"You do live in Winter's Cove? With Hannah Winters?" Mr. Stone asked.

"Well yes, she is my cousin. I am living at her home now."

"Then while you are in school here, you will go by Memory Winters. It is easier on the staff and students when they can associate you with your family." He smiled. "Your family has done a lot for this area and we like to show our appreciation. Now if you will take your seat, you can get started signing all your admission papers. Once you finish, I will assign someone to show you the school and make sure you have no trouble finding your classes. If there is anything, I can do to make the process easier, just let me know."

I was curious about Mr. Stone's unusual behavior, but by noon I had begun to believe it must be a southern thing. All of my teachers went out of their way to make me feel comfortable. Mr. Stone had assigned one of the girls in the class, a petite brunette named Diane, to act as my unofficial guide. Diane seemed friendly enough, but she did not talk unless I asked her a question, and then I had had to ask her to speak up so I could hear her answers. She showed me around the school, making sure I knew where the bathrooms, lockers, library, and break area were. Well the lunch bell rang, she walked with me to the cafeteria. I expected to join her at lunch, but after she picked up her tray, Diane led me to a table full of strangers. At least they were strangers to me, they obviously knew who I was.

"Hi! You must be Memory. We were told you would be joining us today. I am Regina, your cousin. Come sit by me. Move over Dane." She elbowed a cute boy about my age, and he quickly slid over a chair, making room for me to sit by Regina. I nodded my thanks to the boy before I sat down. He returned the nod with a grin before returning to the conversation he'd been having before I walked up.

"How have you been doing today? I guess it has to be hard, moving to a new city three weeks before the summer break. You won't really have a chance to get to know most of the kids until next year." She smiled." Of course, you will soon know all of us. Everyone here at this table is related to you in some way. And we all live in Winter's Cove."

I was puzzled. "Everyone at this table lives in the valley? You all look to be about the same age. What happened? Did all of your parents go to school together, fall in love and decide to have babies at the same time?"

"Something like that. There are one or two still in middle school but most of this generation was born within four or five years of each other. Robert is oldest, he just turned eighteen. Mace, Bryan, Crystal, Hannah and I are the oldest here; we are all sixteen except Bryan. He turned seventeen last month. Dane and Danny the twins, Lisa, and Brent are fifteen like you. Carol, Tony, Amanda, Brent, Coral, and Dawn are fourteen. That's it right now. Cody and Paul are in college, but they will be home in three weeks."

I took my time, studying each face, trying to pick something unique to associate the face with the name as Regina named them off. I hesitated just for a moment at Hannah, who had already left for school before Peggy and I made the trip into town.

Hannah looked exactly like I had pictured her. She had the same features as all of the others; small nose, full lips and darkly fringed eyes in a picture perfect face. She was tall and slim; with long silvery blonde hair just like her mother. But unlike her mother, the look on her face made it clear that she did not welcome me into the family in any way.

"We will have more time to get to know you on the ride home," Regina continued. "And now that you know what we look like, it will be easier for you to spot us. I think Crystal is in your first-period class. Dane and Danny are in your third period. And Dane and Robert are both in your last. Watch them, they will cheat off your paper if they get a chance. They hate economics."

Dane and Danny both smiled, and Robert had winked when I was introduced to him. He was cute; too bad he was a relative. Of course, he might be a cousin so removed that it would not make a difference. I was going to have to look into that.

"Speaking of the ride home, where do I catch the bus? No one mentioned that little detail. Diane is sweet but getting information from her is difficult." *I wondered if she was afraid, she might say the wrong thing?*

"Just meet me at the main door after the bell. We can walk to the bus together. Remember the boys if you get lost, you can follow them to the bus."

I would have loved to ask a few more questions, but the warning bell rang, and everyone hurried to reach their next class before the late buzzer. Diane appeared like magic to guide me but just as she was earlier, she did not talk unless I asked her a question.

For the rest of the day, I was busy trying to adjust to a radically different school environment than the one I was familiar with. For one thing, schools in California required everyone to wear a standard uniform. Here the kids dressed like models, wearing the latest trends from teen fashion magazines. I really stood out in my uniform khaki pants and white pullover. There was nothing designer about them at all. Of course, no one had mentioned the 'no uniform' requirement, not that my own clothes were any better.

Another difference was no Physical Education requirement. Instead, as an elective, I had a jazz dance and exercise class. Another minor detail no one mentioned. I dressed in my green uniform shorts and white blouse, only to find the entire class in leotards and tights. At any other school, I would have been totally humiliated, but surprisingly, no one teased me at all. In fact, no one even made a snarky comment.

In the fifth period, I was having trouble seeing one section of the board over a tall boys head, and one of the girls had moved to the back of the class, offering me her desk without the teacher asking.

It was as if my being associated with the Winters name changed everything. All day long I received the same weird reaction. People made it a point to come up and introduce themselves; offering to show me around the school or asking me if there was anything I needed. I met more people in one day than I knew after an entire school year back in California.

Starting a new school, even for a few weeks, seemed unreal. This time I felt as if I had been jerked out of one world and plopped down into another, completely alien one. The feeling lessened when I actually got into a class and started doing the assignments, but I soon realized that was only a facade. Only one class made me feel as if I was a new student.

I always enjoyed English Lit and Creative Writing, but I had already completed my senior requirements on those subjects. Instead, I was stuck in Geometry, a subject I hated; all the formulas needed to complete the calculations brought on an overwhelming feeling of inadequacy I would never admit to anyone, least of all a bunch of strangers. So of course, they stuck me in the only class I hated more than living among perfect strangers.

I was more than ready when the bell rang signaling a move to my next class. Instead of waiting on Diane, I decided to take a chance and see if I had remembered anything at all. Walking slowly down the unfamiliar hall, I searched for my new locker, but everything still looked the same to me. I was certain there was a pattern somewhere that would help me to find my way around, but so far, I had not discovered it. I stood in the middle of the hall intersection and tried to recognize anything that looked familiar.

A skinny pimply faced girl wearing too much

makeup came up, clutching her books to her bosom and asked me if I needed help finding my locker. I smiled and thanked her when she led me directly to the right one. As she walked away, it occurred to me that I had never mentioned my locker number to the unknown girl.

By the end of the sixth period, I found myself staring at the clock as it ticked down to the end of my first day, hoping I could get out of the building before all the unusual kindness wore off and all the backed up hell broke loose.

The jangling bell signally the end of the final class broke my concentration. It had gone off ten minutes early, but no one seemed to notice.

I could begin to explain how happy I was to see Regina waiting by the door as promised. With Regina leading the way, I followed the small pack of alarmingly similar teenagers heading for a small custom minibus sitting at the head of the line.

"It looks like we are in for some rain," Regina said as we dashed for the bus's open door. "We had better hurry if we don't want to get wet." She explained that the weather in the mountains was changeable in the spring, and prone to heavy summer showers, warning me it might be good if

I carried a small collapsing umbrella in my backpack."

My initial reaction was that this was probably a good idea, but I decided that silence was all the answer Regina expected. Regina seemed to be offering me friendship, but I thought that this was unlikely since Dane had told me earlier that Hannah was her best friend. It was unlikely anyone would be rude to me since I was a relative but as long as Hannah treated me like the unwanted stepsister from Cinderella, I did not expect Regina's kindness to continue much longer. Regina's parents had probably asked her to be nice to her new cousin, and that was all there was to it.

Hannah was seated about halfway to the back of the bus, and Regina made a beeline for the seat straight across the aisle from her. Robert, the cute boy from lunch, was sitting with Hannah, and from the proprietary arm around her shoulder, it was obvious that the two of them were a couple.

So much for that fantasy, I thought wryly. There was an open seat next to Crystal, so I took that one. Maybe Crystal would be willing to consider a new friend? I thought that unlikely but If I had any hope of enjoying even the tiniest bit of normalcy while I was in Winters Cove, I needed to make an attempt.

Everyone on the bus seemed so close, more of an extended family than just friends. No---unless I somehow won over Hannah, there was not going to be much chance for close friendships with any of my cousins.

"Penny for your thoughts?"

Startled, I jumped, almost falling out of my seat. I had been so preoccupied with my poor, poor, pitiful me, I had failed to realize Crystal was talking to me.

"Nothing much; just going over everything I did in my mind and trying to assimilate it all. Today was a lot to take in."

"Here, have chocolate. I always find chocolate the cure for most anything that confounds me."

I smiled. "Chocolate sounds pretty good. I usually grab a coke, empty calories and all, when I am feeling blue." I was feeling better, if Crystal had that much of a sense of humor, there might be a glimmer of hope after all.

I snuck a quick glance at Hannah, hoping for some sign that my cousin was thawing. Hannah's eye remained frosty and cold. But Robert's smile was a heartwarming sign.

CHAPTER 6

SUMMER STARTS

"Drat. Dropped my pencil." I frowned as my last number 2 pencil rolled away from my desk. Inwardly panicking, I twirled the eraser between my fingers and continued observing in vain, praying for it to somehow stop turning over and over until it rolled under a bookshelf near the window and out of my reach. It could not have happened at a worse time. Timed tests were bad enough without having to stop working, get the teachers attention, and hopefully be allowed to either retrieve my lost pencil or borrow one from another student.

Finally, I decided I had no choice but to go after it. I began to raise my hand, knowing that my attempts to retrieve it would distract everyone in the class away from the exam, then hesitated before staring in disbelief as my wayward pencil seemingly reversed its roll, returning by itself to the floor next to my foot.

Never one to look a gift horse in its mouth, I picked up the pencil and returned to my test. Thanks to my unseen benefactor I completed the test with minutes to spare. Silently I whispered a prayer to whatever higher being that was listening. I still did not know who had rolled the pencil my way, but once I found out I would let him or her, know exactly how much I appreciated the assistance.

After two weeks, I had become accustomed to my new life and was no longer looking for a way to escape my imaginary incarceration. I even managed to achieve an uneasy peace with my cousin Hannah. Not that we would ever be best friends, we were frankly too different. Hannah had recently extended what might be considered an olive branch, asking me to join her and a few the others at the lake the upcoming weekend.

I wondered how many non-relatives had ever caught a glimpse of Hannah's softer side. She certainly did not show it at school. In fact, Hannah was the queen bitch at the Murray County High School, and she reveled in it. If she could have figured out a way to get a palanquin into the school, the football team would be carrying it.

It had soon become apparent to me that the Winters clan ruled the school. All of the girls were cheerleaders and all of the boys except Danny played some sport, mostly football and baseball. Danny was the odd one; he was class president as well as captain of the school's chess team. Not that he wasn't athletic, all of my cousins were. It was more of a lack of interest than the ability that kept him from playing. Danny had his mind set on bigger things, it wouldn't be difficult to imagine him in politics. He would excel at it, as he did in everything else. I had no idea why this bugged me, but it did.

Despite our unusual first meeting, Crystal had come to be a tentative friend and confidant. Regina, after her initial '*welcome to the clan*' speech, had reverted to spending all her time stuck up Hannah's ass. Not that she was ever rude; she easily managed to convey that while she did not dislike me, as long as Hannah did not welcome me into their circle, there would be little opportunity for us to become close friends.

Peggy, with advice from Crystal, had taken me shopping in Atlanta, purchasing enough clothes for three people. Along with the requisite blue jeans and t-shirts that everyone wore in the south, I now had an assortment of outfits for school from Hollister, American Eagle, Hurley, and Hot Kiss, as well as more formal dresses, swimwear and some of the most delicate lacy underclothes I had ever seen. I had been in a Victoria's Secret in the mall back in Malibu, but I had never been able to afford to shop there.

The Winters all seemed to be well off, I knew that Hannah spent more money in a week than I had spent in a year back at the foster home. She thought nothing of paying a couple of hundred for a pair of shoes that she might wear once or twice before she donated them to a thrift store in town.

I had also learned a little more about my mothers' family. Both my grandmother and grandfather had passed away, but Crystal's grandmother was my grandmother's sister. And Lisa was the granddaughter of her grandfathers' brother. Her uncle Mattias's grandmother Marie was her grandmother's first cousin. It was a convoluted mess, but it all boiled down to basics. Every male in Winter's Cove was my third or fourth cousin, either by marriage or through direct bloodlines. So if I did decide to date anyone, it would be all right. In fact, to hear Crystal tell it, it would be encouraged.

Not that any of the boys seemed interested in, or even noticed me. People often said I favored my mom, but I didn't really didn't see the resemblance. Maybe in a certain light, if you squinted your eyes and used your imagination you might find a feature or two, we had in common. Same with my dad. I was obviously of Tsalagi descent but having Cherokee blood in the area was not unusual. We were less than an hour from the Reservation.

I looked nothing like my cousins. They looked like a pair of walking, talking Barbie and Ken dolls. I resembled Pocahontas, or I would if she had been born with violet blue eyes. Apparently, bronze skin and ebony hair was not a big turn on. They were all polite but other than a casual remark that might be misconstrued as flirting, I might as well have been invisible.

Today had been slightly different.

I was standing in line in the cafeteria, not really paying a lot of attention to how slowly the line was moving when this stranger stepped in front of me in line. Surprised by his brazen insolence, I stood gaping at him for a few minutes as he filled his tray and then made his way across the room, slipping around the various students to the Winters clan table before casually taking his place in one of the empty chairs…in the vacant chair next to Crystal that was usually mine.

There was something hovering in the back of my mind, some vague memory that hinted of who he was, but at this time I was completely lost about what I should do. There were no empty chairs and I had never sat anywhere except at that table. Finally, with no idea what to do, I approached the table and stood behind him, hoping someone would notice my problem and suggest a solution.

Someone did, just not anyone sitting at the table. I heard a tense "excuse me," and turned, to find three boys standing behind me, each holding a chair.

"Thank you," I said. "Just leave it right there."

My voice must have finally caught the unknown boy's attention. He turned, saw me standing behind him and said, "Can I help you?"

If I was a plant I would have frozen under that icy stare.

"I doubt it," I replied. "You are in my chair."

Crystal slapped him on the shoulder. "Move

down, give Memory some room."

Memory? He appeared startled but shifted his chair, making room for her to sit at the table.

For just a second, I thought I heard Robert saying, "Say hi to your cousin. I'll explain later." Then the tingling stopped, and everyone was talking the same as usual.

"Memory, this rude ass jerk is my brother Cody. He just got home from Georgia Tech and thought it would be fun to drop by and visit his old stomping ground. Just ignore him, he's only scoping out the girls to see if any are worth spending his precious summer vacation with."

No shit? This ass is her brother?

"Yeah," Bryan said, "Kim got married and moved to Ohio. So now he has to make do with the scrubs like the rest of us."

I saw the tiniest twitch of his lips in one corner of his mouth at Bryans' crude statement. This boy would never have to make do, and he knew it. I could already see several of the more popular girls gathering and whispering, their eyes darting to Cody in between giggles and melodramatic hand fans and swoons. Obviously, they thought he was hot. He was good looking, but that ego was a big turnoff. I had no time to nurse some guys fragile ego. I had him pegged already; an athletic rebel, ex-homecoming king who graduated with off the chart SAT scores and was now either the star of the college football team or the class president. The perfect blue-eyed, curly-haired blonde, boy next door. The exact opposite of my ideal man…if there was such a thing.

Face it, if he wasn't Crystal's brother and my third or fourth cousin, I would not have talked to him, and I doubted he would have noticed me.

Well, that's probably not true. He might have me, there were not a lot of girls with my coloring in the area. The Winters Clan ran to blonde hair and blue eyes. All the girls were slender… model thin even. The boys were taller than average and nicely muscled. There were a few deviations, the twins had light brown hair and green eyes, and Paul somehow managed to inherit the dark curly hair of his father but any of them could have graced the cover of a teen magazine. At five eight I was as tall as my female cousins but with my waist length hair, ruddy olive skin and voluptuous curves, I stuck out like a sore thumb. Like most guys, he would be too busy looking at my boobs and butt to notice anything else.

Being a Winters had certain unexpected privileges I had not been prepared for. Like being able to order in delivery on the days I could not stomach another cafeteria meal. There were eight restaurants in town and every one of them delivered to the school. Apparently, they had ordered pizza, and no one had thought to let me know.

Cody took the last bite of his pizza, tossed the crust onto his sister's plate, opened one of the pizza box's and grabbed another slice. If someone had mentioned the availability of a recent delivery, I wouldn't have bothered standing in the salad bar line for so long. Nor did anyone offer me a slice. *I wondered if it was an intentional snub? Too bad*, I thought as I opened the box and helped myself to a slice.

Cody's eyebrow quirked as I took a bite, but it wasn't as if he was going to ask for it back.

No one else seemed to notice.

Crystal seemed oblivious to anything except the person she was texting and everyone else continued their conversations. I sighed, enjoying my minor triumph, and settled down to finish my lunch. When the bell sounded for the next class, everyone scrambled for their things and Cody disappeared without saying another word to me.

The rest of the day seemed to drag on. Even

though it was the final day of the semester it didn't mean that much to me. I had not made many friends in the three weeks I'd been in class and the idea of a summer break at home with Hannah wasn't very appealing.

During the last day of the school year, there was an open house for regional business and colleges to talk to the graduating seniors about future employment or education options. I noticed Bryan and Mace talking to a Marine recruiter about the possibility of enlistment. Since neither needed a job for the money, that seemed like an interesting choice.

Crystal had no interest in the military, but I picked up some info from the recruiting Sargent. For most of my life, I'd believed the only way I could attend college was through a scholarship or the military. I had expected to join up once I graduated, do my six years, three active, three reserves, and go to school. Now that I could afford any Ivy league school I wanted, I was not ready to make that kind of decision.

I was graduating a year ahead of most of the kids because California schools started children at five if they turned six during the school year. Georgia had stopped doing that when the no child left behind law kicked in. Two of my classes were college-level classes and I had a 98 average in both. Now, armed with my 'Go to College' tote bag stuffed with info on the various institutions and an assortment of giveaways, I followed behind Crystal like a puppy following its mama's teat.

Crystal motioned for me to be quiet and follow her through a door in the back of the gymnasium that I'd noticed but never opened before. We hurried down the hall and down a flight of stairs that led to an outside access door. Beyond the door lay the student parking lot.

"Come on! I drove to school today. Let's go to Dairy Queen." She pointed to her black Escalade.

"Sounds good to me." Since DQ was the only restaurant in town that would not deliver, the idea of slipping away for a banana split overcame any of my immediate reservations. No one had noticed our departure, or at least, if they noticed, no one had interfered with our escape. Another benefit of being a Winters. Cutting out an hour before anyone else without having to worry about repercussions was great. The escape plan sounded great right up to the point of finding Mace and Lisa making out in the back seat. Crystal didn't even try to make them stay behind.

The ride home after eating the split was pretty calm. Almost everyone spent their time catching up on all the calls and texts they had missed during the day. Not today, everyone in the SUV was talking. There was an undercurrent of excitement in the air that surprised me. *Did I miss something?*

"What's all the excitement about, it can't be because it's the last day of school," I asked.

Crystal laughed. "It's Friday silly. And Cody's home. Which means Mason will be arriving before dark. What are you wearing to the dance?"

"Dance?" I had no idea what she was talking about.

"Don't tell me no one thought to mention the dance. It's a family tradition. The last weekend of school we always host a dance in the valley. Everyone from school will be there. I've been planning my outfit for weeks."

Great. Please let it not be formal.

"Nope. No one said a word. What are you wearing?" I was mentally going over all the outfits hanging in the closet at home. There were things inside I had no memory of buying. Peggy must have placed them in the cart when I wasn't looking.

"It's adorable. It's teal silk cocktail in a classic cut, but maybe a bit shorter than I usually wear. I found the perfect black and teal strappy heels to wear. They are almost sandals really, or they would be if they were flat. I'm still going back and forth over wearing my hair loose or putting it up with dangly earrings."

"Sounds perfect." And it did. With her coloring teal would be perfect. It was one of my favorite colors. I even had a really cute dress in teal and gold, with tiny gold beads on the bodice. Not that I would dare wear it knowing she would be in teal too."

"What about you?"

"I have absolutely no idea." I didn't. Somewhere in that massive closet, there had to be something suitable.

"Well, I'm sure you will find something. With your body, you could wear a burlap sack and the guys would be falling all over you."

Having a bunch of horny teenage boys pawing at me all night wasn't exactly my ideal evening. Crystal was so excited about the dance but my mind kept flashing back to the Spring Fling, the last dance I had gone to. It was before I was placed at Mrs. Tolbert's. I was living in a group home in L.A., one of the bigger homes that held twenty foster kids at one time.

The County had converted an old church that had been subdivided into rooms for the foster children. The primary room of the building was broken into a kitchen and dining area and a large central gathering room set up with multiple sofas, a couple of computer stations and a large television that was shared by all. The boys and girls each had their own bathrooms, located on opposite sides of the buildings. It was a typical Friday night, most of the younger kids had an eight o-clock bedtime and the teenagers had gathered in the TV area to watch the latest episode of the Vampire Diaries. It had been raining all day and the old church seemed to have issues holding heat in wet weather. Just after the episode got underway, I began to feel chilly. It was April and Ms. Dalton had already packed the winter things away for the season. I tried to keep my mind off the cold but failed. During the first commercial, I decided I had enough time to grab a blanket from storage. The overhead light didn't come on when I flicked the switch to the basement, so I made a mental note to tell Mr. Cooper, the night supervisor when he returned from the drugstore.

After a few seconds, my eyes adjusted enough for me to risk it. I took my time going down the narrow steps, using the hand rail to ensure I didn't stumble in the dark. One of the other kids had fallen down the stairs a couple of months earlier, cracking her collarbone and her right wrist. She was still wearing the cast. The idea of going to school wearing that under my clothes made me shiver, so I was determined not to make the same mistakes she had.

Once I reached the basement floor, I tried the switch again and realized that light didn't work either. I figured the fuse must have blown and modified the report in my mind. My eyes had adjusted by this time and I could see pretty well in the limited light put off by the emergency exit sign at the end of the hall. The storage closet was the door closest to the exit, so it was simple to use the wall as a guide and walk that way.

I paused, listening, convinced I had heard the sound of voices, but after a few seconds, I decided it must have been the television upstairs I had heard.

As I walked in the direction of the storage closet, the distinct sound of masculine and feminine moans reached my ears. Overcome by curiosity, I crept closer, determined to see who was brazenly breaking the house rules. I went over who was missing from the group upstairs, and four or five possibilities came to mind. All of them were older teens and any of them could be brave enough to risk discovery. All were sexually active as far as I knew. As I got closer, I could hear what sounded like a hand against bare flesh— pap…pap….pap….pap! The furnace room door was slightly ajar. Snooping overcome caution and I moved closer to take a peek. Boy, was that a mistake.

The overhead fluorescent lighting made it easy to see Mr. Cooper with his pants down around his knees, standing behind little Mikki. I saw him make a few more quick thrusts before letting out a deep growl and slapping the young girl on her hind end.

When I'd first arrived the social worker had gone on and on about how Cooper was a principled, upstanding citizen; an educated man to whom the State had entrusted many vulnerable children. I'd pretended to listen somehow knowing it was just a skillfully constructed front. I'd seen it many times since entering the system. Instinctively I had known his courteous demeanor and radiant smile masked the wily machinations of a true predator. Mikki might appear to be a willing participant, but at only eleven years old, she might not even realize she was being mistreated. Or it had happened so many times she had become numb to it.

I wanted to say something, but fear of the consequences I would face if he wasn't removed overrode my disgust. I had seen too many kids get the shaft after they reported misconduct and the adult was believed instead of the one being abused. Instead, I inched my way back from the room until I was far enough to turn and tip-toe back upstairs.

Once I was back on the main floor I ran to the bathroom, tears running down my face. Almost as soon as the door closed behind me, I felt the burn of acid as popcorn, coca cola and the remains of the spaghetti I had eaten at dinner splashed into the porcelain bowl. I must have vomited two or three times before I slipped to the ground by the toilet and tried to calm my racing heart. Regina was more than two years younger than I was. It was obvious Cooper had been molesting her for some time, the young girl accepted his advances as if it was expected of her. There was nothing I could do. I washed my hands and face, then reached for a paper towel when I noticed the roll was empty.

"Who uses the last of the paper towel and leaves the empty roll? Shit!" That topped a perfectly screwed up evening.

I had missed at least a third of this week's episode and really didn't want to go back into the main room anyway. To avoid having to answer questions, I went directly to the tiny room I shared with Monique, locked the door and turned out the light. Lying in the darkness I debated myself over whether I should tell someone what I had seen, or stay out of it?

Stay out of it won. Who would I tell?

Ms. Dalton was all right, but she was in her sixties and getting ready to retire. Lately, we were doing well if we saw her once or twice a week. She would not appreciate hearing anything that might rock the boat she was sailing on. She was simply counting down the days until she could move to Florida with her sister.

The rest of the staff were only there to get paid.

Maurice, the custodian, got his job because his

mama and Ms. Dalton attended the same church. Most of the time he was nowhere to be found--- except at meal times, that man could eat more than three teenage boys. He had the bad habit of eating all the residents' snacks and then letting one of the younger kids take the blame. No one would be surprised to hear he had fallen into a diabetic coma.

Maurice was one of those men you instinctively knew to avoid when you saw him coming your way. To be honest, I was surprised that he wasn't the one abusing Mikki. Except, from the way he watched the younger boys, I figured his tastes ran along a different path than Coopers.

Ms. Paula spent most of her time on the phone, too caught up in her love triangle to care for her charges. We could pretty much do anything we wanted to do when she was in charge. That's when we slipped out to go hang with the normal kids. All you had to do was wait until she made her bed check rounds and then slip out the door while she was on the phone. By law, they could not lock the front door, since there had to be ways to escape a fire in an emergency. So we had no problems getting in or out of the building.

The kitchen staff never spoke to the kids at all.

No one would give a flying fug about any of us. They were both Latino and had at least four kids each. Each day they took all the leftovers home with them. I wouldn't be surprised if they cooked extra just to ensure there would be plenty to take with them at the end of the day. On the weekends they would bring the kids to work with them and let them spend the day playing with the younger kids in the house. Even if we told them about Cooper, they would not say anything.

For the time being, I decided to keep my mouth shut about what I'd seen—figuring as long as Cooper was focused on Mikki, he wouldn't be thinking about the other girls. I'd noticed the way he'd looked at me when he thought no one was looking. He hadn't made any overt sexual advances, but I'd recognized the look in his eyes. I'd seen it many times since I'd started developing. Now I had had real validation for my uncomfortable feeling. And despite my fear, guilt was eating at me.

During the next week, the feeling of impending doom grew stronger. Since I'd been placed at the group home, new kids arrived and departed almost daily. In fact, there were two new boys in the day room this morning.

I wished they would move me. Ms. Dalton was retiring at the end of the month and Mr. Cooper would be taking over as House Director. Just last night he had insinuated things would be changing once he took over. He stopped me in the hall and struck up a conversation, one I'd had been dreading.

"Now that I'm going to be in charge, it will give me more of an opportunity to get to know you one on one." He allowed his eyes to rove over my body as if he was already assured of my compliance.

Watching his face shift into a lascivious leer, I felt a shiver of disgust run down my spine.

"That won't be necessary, Mr. Cooper."

"Necessary or not I'm looking forward to our time together."

He took a step toward me and I stepped back one. He laughed. "It's a cold, cold world, young lady….especially for one as uppity as you. It will benefit you to learn now how to appreciate the advantages of having a friend in power."

"What's that supposed to mean?"

He licked his lips. "I've read your file… You're a smart girl…figure it out. I'm sure if you wrapped your head around it…you could come up with something that would make both of us happy."

Mr. Cooper was changing the rules. I was now certain he desired to "know" me intimately, just as he knew Mikki. That was not going to happen. I might not be able to save her, but I would be damned if I was going to walk into the lion's den like a scared lamb. It wasn't in my DNA.

"One girl isn't enough for you?" I asked.

His eyes narrowed.

That's when I realized I had made a serious mistake.

His eyes grew black and cold, and he seemed to be having difficulty breathing. His skim flushed and seemed to get redder by the minute. I had no idea what he had in mind, but I was certain it would not be good for me.

I did not wait for him to collect himself, I ran for the main room, joining three other kids in a game of rummy.

He stood at the door watching me but did not say anything. We both knew the secret and he intended to ensure I never told anyone. It would be lights out soon, and he had a key to every lock in the building. Overcome by desperation, I began to go over every possible scenario. Nothing ended with me a winner.

Less than an hour later all hell broke loose, and I didn't have anything to do with. Perhaps it was Karma. Or perhaps God heard my prayer and actually decided to say yes.

Mikki had not been feeling well all day. After complaining her stomach hurt too much to eat, she had been excused from dinner. Ms. Paula had called the doctor to come to the center, and she was sitting on the sofa beside Mikki, letting the girl rest her head in her lap while she texted her boyfriend.

Mikki suddenly decided she needed to go to the bathroom. Ms. Paula waved her on, and she headed across the room. She made it four or five steps when she stopped and screamed. Blood was pouring down her legs, forming a scarlet puddle on the ground by her feet.

"Someone grab me some towels," Ms. Paula screamed as she snatched up the screaming girl and laid her out on the sofa. The first towel was soaked through in minutes. She exchanged the bloody cloth for a dry towel, placing it under Mikki while holding the second against her loins.

One of the boys had run to find Mr. Cooper. The night supervisor arrived seconds behind the

Doctor. Dr. Patrick knew what had happened as soon as he saw Mikki. Instead of asking questions, he inserted an I.V. line, started fluids and gave her an injection while waiting on the ambulance he'd ordered to arrive. His eyes moved from boy to boy around the room, searching for evidence of guilt. He was surprised that none of the young men seemed uncomfortable or guilt-ridden.

This would have been the perfect time for me to say something. I was so angry that no one appeared to realize what had been going on right before their eyes. I took a step toward the doctor.

Cooper wouldn't take his eyes off me. He stared across the room; lips pressed tight together and livid eyes clamped onto mine. He was daring me to open my mouth and I knew it. My heart was pounding, and it became hard to catch my breath.

Dr. Patrick was watching me from the corner of his eyes as if he realized I knew something that I wasn't saying. I was about to call him a soulless bastard and rat him out when all the lights went off.

Another blackout.

Even the backup generators failed to kick in. We were sent to bed since there was nothing we could do without power. I wanted to make sure Cooper wasn't left in charge while Ms. Paula dealt with the hospital.

Karma was on my side because Mr. Cooper accompanied Dr. Patrick to the hospital. As soon as they left, I thought about telling Ms. Paula what I knew, but fear of repercussions overcame me. I did the sensible thing instead, I locked my door, jammed a broom handle across the threshold to prevent it from being opened, got into bed and went to sleep.

Ms. Paula called us all into the great room the next morning. Mikki had died a few hours later, they were not able to stop the hemorrhage after she lost the baby. She was going to be cremated, so they allowed us to visit the funeral home that afternoon. It didn't seem real, they had dressed the body in a really nice dress, one obviously donated by a wealthy sponsor of the group home. Mikki would never have worn something pink and preppy. On her feet, they had placed white lace socks and loafers. She would have been happier in jeans and her high tops. It was an obvious show to gain donations. *How could someone turn the tragedy of her death turned into a marketing scheme to gain new financial sponsors? Didn't anyone care about her being molested?*

Mr. Cooper's eyes never left me the entire time we were in the funeral home as if he knew what I had planned to do. He was warning me to keep my mouth shut. I knew I was going to catch hell, but I didn't care anymore. I was going to tell everything I knew.

After we returned from the funeral home, we were all called into the main room for a house meeting. The director of Child Services informed us that the home would no longer house boys and girls. All the girls were told they were being moved to new foster homes. They had already made the arrangements for transfer. The van would be there in less than an hour. We were dismissed to pack our things and be ready to leave.

Immediately.

I sighed and headed for my room. It took me less than a quarter hour to throw my things into the old cardboard case and report to the transport van.

That was home number nine since I'd had become a ward of the court. I often wondered if Cooper was molesting the little boys now. Maybe that was why I had so many bad dreams. Guilt built up for not speaking out about the monster on the staff. I hoped not because there was no way I could ever make that right. Karma had taken care of Cooper, I had heard on the news he'd been involved in an eight-car accident after falling asleep at the wheel while under the influence. He was still alive but had damaged his spinal cord. He would never get sexually abuse another little girl the way he did Mikki.

I swallowed, forcing down the nervous acid that burned the back of my throat and commanded my stomach to keep calm, even though my heart was pounding wildly. I was so tired of pretending I was happy being alone. All I wanted to do was find someone that would care for the person I was, once I peeled away all the false layers, I had wrapped myself in.

There was a chance someone in the area could be that person. Only time would tell. It wasn't that I didn't believe in destiny, it was just that I believed destiny often needed a really hard shove.

Back home I always had boys around. Most were just good friends, but every so often I'd found one I wanted to spend more time with. So far three had actually been called my boyfriend in public. Truth was, I really needed to think about changing my love life, or lack of one.

After two weeks at the new school, I had realized there were a few downsides to being related to the Winters clan that no one had thought to mention. The boys were scared to talk to me. Most of the girls were scared, too. Not that they were mean. If anything they were overly polite and helpful. It was *children of the corn* eerie.

I didn't really understand why people I'd just met assumed I was anything like the rest of the Winters clan. I guess that's what happens when you spend most of your time with the same people. Since that had never been a consideration until now, I could only make a thoughtful guess. Either way, I was determined to enjoy myself at the End of the Year dance, since I was being forced to attend it.

My history with dances was not good. I sighed and prayed that tonight's dance would not be anything like the last one. I was finally beginning to feel at home.

CHAPTER 7

DANCE

The clock said 7:58 PM when Crystal pulled her Cadillac Escalade into the circled driveway leading to the house. When she got out, I was hit by a flood of doubt, immediately second guessing my choices. The teal one shoulder cocktail dress she was wearing was adorable. It was the perfect foil for her pale blonde hair and creamy peach complexion.

Not that I could imagine one of the Winters clan ever being anything except perfect. I was actually feeling pretty good myself. At the back of the closet, tucked down behind the new clothes my aunt had purchased, I had discovered a cream-colored tunic of loosely woven cotton that looked like silk and was long enough to wear as a mini dress over a nude body stocking. I debated wearing the matching trousers but decided, what the hell. It was a dance and I was tired of feeling dowdy around my cousins. The combination gave the illusion I wasn't wearing anything under the dress while providing complete coverage. The addition of dangly silver earrings, a thin silver rope necklace, and the strappy white and silver heeled sandals that were all that remained of my Pepto pink nightmare, completed the look. Instead of braiding my hair or wearing in pulled back in a horse's tail, I had used a curling iron to add soft waves and left it loose. The best part was I looked nothing like the other women in the Winters clan.

Crystal was grinning as she slid into the SUV. "Damn girl, you look hot. I would never be able to pull off that outfit. Let's go. I can't wait to see the look on everyone's face when you walk in"

***

The dance was well underway when we arrived. The parking field was packed, easily holding over four hundred vehicles in temporary rows laid out with flour. The white flour lines would last until the next good rain unless the birds and insects carried it off beforehand.

Crystal was right, everyone in school was there. Someone had arranged for both a live cover band and a disc jockey to keep the music going at all times. The heavy bass beat of the music got my heart pumping long before we reached the brightly lit horse arena. The caterers had rolled a series of heavy s down atop most of the horse show area to provide a walking surface. Tables and chairs were scattered around the back half and both sides up to the edge of the dance floor. Crystal said the stage and dance flood was a modular system that came apart for storage. That way it could be used year after year without having to build a new one each time. Everywhere I looked there were teenagers, many dressed in cocktail and after five attire, others in jeans and t-shirts, depending on their mood or financial situation.

My stomach was full of butterflies and not a one was staying still. My record with dances was not the best and the flashback dreams I'd experienced during the previous night only increased my trepidation. *What if no one asked her to dance?*

It soon became evident that wasn't going to be a problem.

It was crazy. We had just enough time to reach a table in the family area and drop our things before we were engulfed by a swarm of eager young men (and two young women) all wanting a partner for the next dance.

"It's a tradition," Crystal whispered as she pasted a welcoming smile on her face, "you dance with anyone that asks. No excuses. Just go with it."

Seemed like a perfectly fine idea to me. I had to admit the sight of the petite blonde goddess being dragged toward the crowded dance floor by a wheezing, extremely rotund young man with bright red hair, made me smile.

I felt a hand on my shoulder and turned, seeing a boy from my math class at school standing behind me.

"Dance?" He asked. Despite the awkward shift of his weight from foot to foot, he was cute. I wondered what I had done to make him feel insecure. I had never noticed anyone having that problem before.

"Sure." We moved off to the throbbing beat of Immaterial. The deejay seemed to be enjoying himself, switching from the pop song to the soothing country lyrics of Sam Hunts' Backroad to the latest gift from Gaga. No one cared what was playing as long as the beat emanating from the speakers was both loud and on point.

I noticed a couple of the girls didn't seem to be enjoying themselves as much as some of the others. It only took four songs to figure out what it was. Being black in the white-dominated Tennessee mountains had to be hard enough. To be both black, and gay, had to be next to impossible.

I decided to liven things up a bit. What the hell, all they could do is throw me out of the family. I'd survived DFACS in Los Angeles, nothing I'd seen so far in Georgia intimidated me, much less actually scared me.

As soon as Gaga made the last swallow, I headed for the DJ's booth and made my request.

"Are you sure? I'd hate to lose my gig over this." He said it, but he was already digging through his cd collection as he spoke.

"I got you, play the song, no one will say anything." As the first beats of Post Malone's Rockstar came from the speakers, I held my hand out, signally for the two girls, inviting them to join me the dance floor. Their eyes lit up as they recognized the song. One cocked her eyebrow a bit but the smile she offered me was worth every bit of the bullshit I was expecting to receive once the lyrics of the song became apparent to my new family.

The kids on the floor went wild. The floor quickly because too crowded to do little more than a simple bob and weave. Twerking was evident everywhere, but very little actual dancing. Nobody cared.

My new family surprised me. I saw my aunt shift uncomfortably in her chair, but she didn't open her mouth. Most of my cousins were already on the floor and they moved smoothly from the bouncy pop to the harder hitting street music. The Deejay quickly followed the first song up with Electricity and El Bano. When he slowed it down with Love Lies, I begged off and headed back to the table to catch my breath. After I made a quick detour to the bathroom, I stopped long enough to grab some punch and a plate of hot wings and then collapsed at the table.

"That was you, wasn't it?" Cody asked as he slid into the next chair.

I squirmed uncomfortably for a moment and then figured what could he do?

"Guilty. I couldn't handle one more high-pitched squeal from the latest pop princess. Well, I do like Havana, but they can only play it so many times in one night. And the Deejay only brought a few country songs. Besides, don't they look like they are having a good time now?"

It was kinda weird, discussing this with Crystals brother. I'd been in the family for less than two weeks and had just begun to relax my natural guards around them. Only Crystal had become somewhat of a friend. So why did I feel so comfortable around her brother?

I thought about heading back to the dance floor, but I didn't want to ruin the chance of a perfectly good, and reasonably intelligent conversation. It might never happen again.

"Hell yeah. I was about to find a spot to hide out until the band started back. If I heard one more bubble gum pop song. I was expecting Bieber Fever or something worse at any time."

I tried to keep the look of amazed shock off my face. It seemed that underneath the hard-ass attitude was an actual walking, talking, normal human being. If he could be real; maybe I had been wrong about some of the others too.

I sighed as the Deejay slipped in the perfect slow dance song. I always had loved Ed Sheeran. It must have shown in my eyes because Cody grinned and pulled me to my feet.

"Well, then I guess this is my dance. Come on,

you can't turn me down…rules are rules."

I shrugged and let Cody lead me to the dance floor. *It would be a slow dance,---a romantic slow dance. And I was dancing with a person I had only met once before. Not only that, he was some kind of distant cousin. Was that even legal? He didn't feel like a cousin...*

"Relax," he whispered, leaning his head close to my ear. "It's still early. You're doing great." His hand slid down my back and he pulled me close against him before he moved into complicated quickstep. I closed my eyes and let my body follow his, mentally thanking my music teacher who had thought it important that everyone in the class learned the basics of waltz and the other classical partner dances.

As the final strains of the music died, Cody released me with a last whirl and dip, like an old Fred Astaire movie. I was disappointed. It had been so long since anyone had held me in their arms that way, I didn't want to let that feeling go.

"It's alright, he said with a grin. You're free to go now." He held his hand out to the same brunette I'd seen him dancing with earlier. I hadn't noticed her approach, but she'd obviously noticed us. The look in her eyes made my skin crawl. Cold blooded bitch, I'd seen snakes with warmer expressions.

"Um, thanks," I replied, unsure whether I should just walk back to the table or wait for the floor to open up, so I could slide into the abyss below. I was certain there was a level of hell located directly beneath the dancefloor, filled with the humiliated remains of starstruck young women who'd been left standing on the dancefloor.

Once again, the Deejay came to my rescue, putting an old favorite line dance song that I was really good at. I fell into line beside two other girls and before I knew it, everyone was working their way through the cupid shuffle.

By the time the next song started my dance card was once again full and Cody and his rather interesting friend were nowhere to be found.

*****

Crystal slid into the driver's seat and tossed her jacket and purse into the back seat of her Escalade. She waited as I got situated before pulling out into the stream of cars exiting the rapidly emptying arena.

"Well what did you think of your first family event?" she asked.

"It was fun. Are all of them like this?"

Crystal laughed. "No, thank goodness. Most are simple family get-togethers. A dinner, barbeque, birthday party, you know, the normal things. We do spend a lot of time together, but that's probably because we all live here in the valley."

"So we have a whole summer…what is there to do?"

"Girl, you sound so pathetic. There's plenty to do here. Besides the obvious horses, which I'm sure you noticed tonight, we have a fantastic lake. Do you ski?"

"Nope. I surf."

"Not much opportunity for surfing here. But we do have jet skis. And boogie boards. We even have some of the water jets, but the boys seem to like them more than the girls. They like to do tricks in the air. Paul broke his arm last year, showing off."

"Why'm I not surprised?"

"We can hit the lake tomorrow if you like. You did bring your suit, right?"

CHAPTER 8

LAKE

Not again! I grabbed a tissue and dabbed at my eyeliner, wiping off the shakily drawn line. No matter how hard I tried, I could not get the line thin enough. Snatching the jar of cold cream off the counter, I cleaned away the latest attempt. Now only a tiny smudge remained to remind me of the previous five aborted attempts. Sighing, I carefully drew the liner brush across the lid of my eyes, deftly flicking upwards at the corners. My hand remained sure and steady this time. Not willing to further add to my irritation over my five tragic attempts to add waterproof liner; I confidently added another coat of waterproof mascara to my lashes. I was going to the lake, not a night club so why was I so worried about it being perfect?

The pounding at the bathroom door broke my train of thought.

"Memory! Crystal is waiting on you. Hurry

up." Hannah was in her usual warm and loving state of mind, somewhere between tasteless tepid and frozen solid with no hope of survival.

"Sorry," I replied as I softened my face into a semblance of a smile for my loving cousin. For some reason, Hannah had disliked me from the moment we met, and things had not improved over time. Since I had no idea why she felt that way, I had given up on ever becoming friends and learned to be satisfied with barely cordial. At least she was speaking to me, for the first week she hadn't said a word. Not that she was any less of a bitch, but at least I got my messages. I practiced deep breathing for a few seconds before opening the door.

"Thanks for letting me know," I called out as I headed for the staircase. I didn't wait for my cousin to reply. Too bad I couldn't shut out the voices in my head as easily. Once again, I worried that something might be seriously wrong with me. I'd read somewhere online that one of the symptoms of a tumor in the brain was smelling weird odors, seeing things that were not there or hearing voices.

Maybe I should mention it to my aunt? No, aunt Peggy was not much better than Hannah. It made me wonder why they had gone to so much trouble to find me. It obviously wasn't because they wanted me there. Maybe Marie did, but Peggy ruled the household like Hannah ruled the school. Uncle Matt did his best to make me feel wanted, but it was obvious he could care less either way.

I was really looking forward to hitting the lake. Crystal had been out of town for three days with her family, so I did not have anyone to hang with. I was sick of sitting in my room playing video games or reading. I had watched the entire run of Weeds and started in on Riverdale.

Ever since the End of School Dance, I had been looking forward to visiting the lake. According to Crystal, the family owned their own private beach and an assortment of water toys that anyone in the family was welcome to use. I had never been on a jet ski and my heart was set on experiencing that little bit of joy as soon as possible. It was something I'd wanted to try for ages. Of course, life in a foster care program did not include things like ski boats and jet skis. The only reason we got to go to the beach was because it didn't cost the government anything except the gas we used in the van. We could pack 15 in the van easily, so it only took one to get us there most of the time.

Crystal appeared just as eager to go swimming, but most of that was the idea of getting her boyfriend into swim trunks. Like all of the other male cousins, he sported the ideal vee shaped muscular torso and washboard abs. And of course, he was into outdoor sports, so he had a fantastic tan to go with that body.

We had to make a detour into town to pick up a package for Crystal's mother that was waiting at the post office. While we were in town, I convinced her to stop by the local Wally World, so I could grab a jar of my favorite cocoa butter and a new pair of sunglasses. I had to admit, having money to buy something I wanted when the urge hit me, instead of saving for weeks to get it, was fantastic.

"I have no idea why you need tanning butter; your skin is already twice as dark as anyone else in the family."

"Because my skin dries out in the sun and this keeps me from peeling. You should try it, you would look fantastic with darker skin." I pictured her looking like Malibu Barbie and couldn't help but smile. They were all so perfect, I felt fat and dumpy around them. The sad thing about that was I was actually considered underweight for my height. I had a curvy figure, with full breasts and a well-rounded rear. All my cousins looked like they could step on a runway in Paris without worrying about whether the clothes would fit.

"I'll stick to the tanning beds for now. Between that, and a good spray tan, I don't have to spend all my time lying still in the sun. I enjoy the water too much and I would have to be constantly replying it."

"I think I'll stay with natural, tanning beds scare me. Of course, that could be because I saw someone get cooked inside one in a movie, I watched a few years ago." I never understood why the group homes were always showing horror movies. Maybe they were trying to show life in the homes wasn't so bad?

"Remind me to check into your SCUBA certification," Crystal added. We take a family trip to the Caribbean every winter. There's nothing like diving the crystal clear waters off the islands."

"Swim under the water? I worked really hard to learn how to stay on top of the water."

"Trust me. You will love it. And there are always so many good looking guys on the ship."

"Hmmm. The truth comes out. You just need a

wingman while you're prowling for new meat."

"You are so bad. Don't you ever think about guys?" She suddenly paled. "Wait! I never thought to ask. You're not gay or you? I just assumed because you were family you would like men as much as me."

"Relax. I'm not gay," I replied.

"Bi?"

"Nope. Straight as a ruler."

"Thank heavens. I was worried I had just stuck my foot in my mouth. Coral is gay. She mentioned she didn't get a lesbian vibe when talking to you, but she wished she had. I guess it's easy to miss the signs. Cody had a friend from school who is gay, and he got a big crush on Cody. Cody missed it completely. It broke the boy's heart when he found out Cody considered him simply as one of the guys. He quit school the next day and Cody felt rotten about it for months."

"Well, that won't be a problem with me. I like big, strong, muscular guys with brains and a great sense of humor. Unfortunately, they are few and far between."

"What about your cousins? They all fit the description."

I laughed. "I am still trying to learn the rules

of conduct in the family. You take things for granted, while I have to think about everything I say or do. It's been easier to avoid the boys until I figure out the guidelines."

"Well, if any of the boys in the cove interest you, go for it. None of them are close enough relations to prevent you from dating. Well, if Hannah was a boy, you couldn't date her, but that's about it."

"I'll try to control my disappointment."

We both broke out laughing and were still giggling like little girls when we arrived at the Marina.

We parked in a small private lot beside a private marina and made our way over to the beach. Sometime in the past, one of my ancestors had spent a big chunk of money trucking in enough white sand to create a picture-perfect beach. It stretched along the shoreline about a quarter of a mile and was a good two hundred feet deep. While my family didn't own the entire lake, they did own a good percentage of it. And the other owners had no complaints since the Winters family spend a lot of money maintaining perfection.

The water was kept up by a private management company that stocked the lake with game fish and regulated the water table so that it was always kept at the perfect depth. Every day, a crew of four men swept the shoreline in a vacuum boat to ensure the water and surrounding land was as clean as a public lake could be. They also paid a private group to go into the public park and clean up twice a week, on Monday and Friday.

The private area was even better.

There was a permanent volleyball net set up on the beach and two large floating docks about a hundred feet from shore. One of the floating docks had a slide and the other had a floating trampoline attached to it. I watched as one of the twins climbed up a metal platform, and then jumped off, hitting the trampoline and bouncing up into a twisting summersault before returning to the water in a perfect dive. One of the girls was cheering him on, but I could not tell which one it was from the shore.

Cody, Tony, and the other twin were playing Paul, Bryan, and Brent in a volleyball match.

We walked past them to Crystal's favorite spot and spread out the two big quilts she carried around in the trunk of her car. Almost as soon as we had dropped the bags, Mace appeared. He grabbed Crystal around the waist from behind in a bearhug, swinging her up and around in a circle, before dropping her on the quilt and falling to the ground beside her.

I did my best to pretend they were not there for the next few minutes. Once they came up for air, Mace said, "Hey Mem. How's it going?"

"Just fine. How has your day been?"

"Lonely. I didn't think you guys would ever get here. What took you so long? Crystal got another boyfriend I don't know about?"

"What makes you think you're my boyfriend?" Crystal hated to be taken for granted but she also really liked Mace.

"But…" Mace looked like she had just stolen his tootsie pop and taken a big bite.

His expression reminded me of a little boy who had just found out there was Santa Clause.

Crystal saw his face fall and melted. "Come here silly." She pulled him onto her arms and kissed him again. "I was just teasing. We had to go by the post office for mama. She's been waiting on this package for weeks. Then we had to drop it by the house before we could come. So we went in a big circle."

"Dang. I figured it was something like that." Along with the kiss Crystal had given him back his confidence. He pulled a long strand of grass from a patch growing near a rosebush and was tickling her with the tip.

Crystal slapped at his hand every time he got too close to her breasts but other than that, pretty much ignored his efforts.

Once again, I felt like a third wheel. Simply hanging out, goofing around, and having a conversation wasn't the same when there were three of them. Not that Mace wasn't a lot of fun. He was. I simply preferred not having to have to fight to get Crystals' attention. So I stayed to myself as much as possible and let them enjoy the others company.

Besides, who could blame Crystal for preferring Mace's company? He was hot. *Face it girl... you are jealous. Crystal had a life, a boyfriend, real friends... and I was just a tag-a-long charity case. At least she's isn't moaning and groaning about Michael like the other girls.*

"Hey! Heads Up!"

I looked up at Cody's call, just in time to avoid getting hit by a wild ball Paul had spiked. Instead of going over the net, it had taken a wild turn and flew backward toward our quilts, coming extremely close to hitting both the cuddling couple and me.

Cody trotted along its flight path, trying to retrieve it before it rolled down the slope into the lake. A slight crease appeared between his brows when he turned and saw his sister and Mace clutched in a fervent embrace.

He shot the ball at them like he would shoot a basket, bouncing it off the back of Mace's head.

"Break it up, bonehead. Don't want to give the kiddies ideas." When Mace offered him a five-fingered salute, he ignored him and dropped to the quilt, determined to torture them into what he considered proper public behavior. He smiled at me and began bouncing the ball off the back of his friend. About the third bounce, Mace gave up.

"All right. You win. No more making out on the beach."

"Don't I get a say-so in this matter?" Crystal wasn't really mad, but she hated to give her brother the satisfaction of even his tiny win.

"Nope." He was openly grinning now. He turned to me and winked.

I couldn't help but grin back.

"Hey, Memory." Cody was feeling nervous now, but he had no idea why. Normally when he flirted with a girl she responded by flirting back.

Memory, on the other hand, acted like she could not wait to get away from him. He had no idea why; he was certain she wasn't gay.

Crystal was watching her brother and her new cousin. Cody was only a couple of years older but at times he seemed like an old man. When he wasn't joking around, he became entirely too serious. Like now. His eyes were intense; as if talking to Memory at the lake was a matter of utmost importance. That was interesting. Was her brother interested in Memory? That would be an interesting match. She wondered how she could manipulate things to make it happen.

Then a horn blew from the direction of the parking lot, and everyone turned to see who it was.

***

I pulled my eyes away from Cody's to see who laying on the horn. When I saw the red BMW convertible pulling into an empty spot, dread washed over me. *Hannah…damn.*

My cousin wasn't mean or anything, she simply made me feel as if I wasn't quite as good as the others were. Straightening my slumping shoulders, I inhaled, telling myself to calm down. I had to keep my paranoia tamped down to a reasonable level, hysteria over Hannah joining her family at the lake was blowing things way out of proportion. Now was the time to remain cool-headed and just have fun. Blanking any sign of insecurity from my expression, I forced myself to widen my smile and relax. Before I could open my mouth and stick my foot in, Crystal, always one to assert herself, announced. "Shit! The bitch is here."

"Quick, someone get a bucket of water; maybe she will melt," Cody said.

I put my hand over my face, fighting down the laugh waiting behind my clenched teeth upon hearing Cody's verbal response to my own personal opinion.

Of course, Hannah would show up. She probably followed us to see where we were going. I often wondered if my cousin got her jollies from making my life miserable.

She was something of an enigma. Take my allowance for example. My aunt Peggy paid for all my necessities and then gave me an extra fifty dollars every week, a type of mad money I had never experienced before arriving in Georgia. For the first two weeks, Hannah made subtle snide remarks whenever no one was around about her parents ensuring I didn't look like little orphan Annie. It wasn't until the third week that I found out it was my own money they were passing out to me, not their generosity. In fact, on paper, I was wealthier than they were…or I would be when I came of age. Despite multiple requests, I had not received a real answer as to when that would be. The closest thing I got to an answer was sometime after my sixteenth birthday. On August 17th I would be sixteen, so I would have an answer one way or another, by the time we returned to school.

Too bad Regina was out of town, she was the only girl in the family that wasn't afraid of Hannah. Even Crystal tended to fawn all over her when she held court, and her royal high-ass considered any location she honored with her presence, her kingdom.

Going by the way all the boys were behaving, they didn't disagree. They were acting like a pack of puppies gamboling around their masters' feet as she walked along the path to the water. Too bad there was no way to show them all exactly how little Hannah cared about their feelings. Not that they would believe it.

The truth was…as much as I hated having the

royal bitch show up everywhere, Hannah had more of a right to be there than I did. She grew up in the Cove, I was the intruder. If only I could stand hanging around with her. After multiple attempts to carry on a normal conversation about umpteen different subjects, only to find out she was laughing about my accent and public school education behind my back, I gave up. Hannah would never be my friend. She tolerated my presence in the house because she had no other alternative.

Crystal suggested I should try and talk to Aunt Peggy about my misgivings, but there was no way I would ever consider discussing Hannah with her mother. Just thinking about how my aunt would react, exhausted me. It was better to accept the facts and learn how to deal with it.

As usual, my dear cousin Hannah was perfectly groomed. Today she had every golden blonde hair slicked into place and it would probably stay that way despite the breeze off the water. In comparison, I had simply pulled my own waist-length brown hair into two long braids and tied them with twists. When it dried, it would form loose waves. I loved that I wouldn't have to use a curling iron to whip it into some kind of style, unlike when I washed it and let it dry naturally. Then, no matter how much I combed and sprayed, without a flat iron to control the frizz, stray locks would always escape to curl along my hairline.

She was wearing a gorgeous Hawaiian print two-piece swimsuit with a bandeau top and boy cut shorts. I would have looked ridiculous on me, but it hung perfectly on her lanky body. With my curves, I needed more support, so I avoided strapless anything, especially something that could come off in the water at any time. Nor would I dare to wear a black, red and yellow print. It reminded me of the story of the country mouse and the city mouse, except in this case the country mouse had it all together, and the city mouse looked like something the cat dragged in.

Of course, once Hannah arrived, I could be walking around naked and no one would have noticed. It was still too strange, a month ago I had no family at all, now I had a large extended one. And these were all my cousins, even though most were third or fourth cousins or more removed. And of course, I was out of place in the group… again.

As Hannah settled back into her beach chair to watch the volleyball game, the boys began to show off; spiking balls, making jump shots and generally doing anything to catch her attention. A couple of the boys were horsing around, shoving each other. Hannah shot them a forceful glare, allowing a faint crease to show between her perfect brows and sudden stillness descended. It was apparent she was the queen of the cove, in school and out.

As if she had heard my thoughts, she shifted her weight putting a hand over her eyes like a visor and stared at me, her eye contact unwavering. I had to force myself not to check for something out of place.

Cody turned all one hundred watts of his charm on, winking at Hannah, treating her to the same winsome looks she used to get her way when she wanted something. And right this moment, it was obvious she wanted attention. Since Robert wasn't at the lake, I guess she figured Cody would make an attractive, …and available, substitute.

I didn't understand how she did it. Hannah was pretty, but so was every other girl in the family. They all could be body doubles for Barbie. What made her so attractive to the guys? It wasn't her warm and generous personality. She could freeze an inferno with one look.

I was still musing when I heard Dane and Danny talking to Hannah. They were the same age as me, more or less, but neither had gone out of their way to make me feel welcome. I wasn't sure which one of them was speaking. The twins were not identical but similar enough to each other in looks, that I could not tell the difference yet. Even their voices were similar, and I hadn't known them long enough to pick up the little nuances that would indicate which one was speaking. Alone they were fine, but when they were together, they would start and end each other's sentences, and that made listening to some conversations downright eerie.

Today they had been decent. Not especially welcoming, but no obvious snubs either.

Were they all patronizing me? Or was I being petty because Hannah was there? It was something I needed to figure out.

I had begun to look at living in the Cove as a second chance. An unexpected opportunity to move beyond my past and work toward being something more than an orphaned girl in the system. I had one year of high-school left and then I could look forward to college.

College! It had never been on my radar before. My grades were okay but nothing spectacular, so I'd given up hope for a scholarship long ago. Education is expensive and with no money, I had resigned myself to some type of menial, minimum wage job. Now, I could afford to go to any college I chose to attend, and there was no reason to worry about being able to afford it. US-CAL had popped into my mind, but I had to discard that idea almost immediately. No, if I went to college, it would be somewhere much closer to home, not clear across the country at the University of Southern California.

I sighed. Home… It was starting to feel like home here. In four short weeks, I had begun the transformation from a penniless orphan into a member of the Winters clan. All I had ever wanted was a normal life. Some fun. Even a bit of flirting. Now I had it and I was spending most of my time waiting to wake up.

***

Catty bitch. Yes! That fit. There are many words I could use to describe my cousin Hannah, but 'nice' wasn't one of them. Scratch off loving, caring, warm, considerate and thoughtful from the list too. I had no idea why I was upset, but there was something about the way she was fawning over Cody that struck me the wrong way. It bothered me more than sitting next to Crystal and Mace while they were making out.

Right now, all I needed was to put some distance between me and the new couple, so that I could get my emotions under control. I looked around and spotted a narrow path winding upward along a small bluff and decided to explore. Walking would take my mind off her obvious seduction attempt and give me an opportunity to destress without anyone realizing how upset I was. I started walking faster.

There was something restful about being alone in the woods, simply chilling and soaking in the silence. Well, not exactly silence, there were plenty of birds singing, and I could hear the rustle of something small, like a squirrel, or a raccoon moving through the underbrush nearby. Somewhere in the distance, someone was barbecuing, the enticing scent of smoking meat and hickory occasionally wafted through the air. I realized I was hungry and wondered if anyone had thought to bring a snack. Crystal had rushed me out before I had a chance to eat breakfast, and the banana I had snatched off the counter on my way out the door was not cutting it. I needed food, soon.

The trail I was following opened out to a man-icured picnic pavilion, complete with a table, small grill, and best of all, a porch-type swing set up to overlook an unparalleled view of the lake. It was perfect.

I collapsed onto the swing, and closed my eyes, enjoying the sense of peace all around me. This was possibly the first time I had been totally alone in the last six weeks. Looking back, other than when I was in bed asleep, someone had been with me at all times. Not obviously so, but now that I was thinking about it, there was always someone nearby. Recently it had been Crystal more than anyone else, but even around the house, Peggy or Matt and even Hannah seemed to stay within calling distance. Everyone here went to the same school, the same church and shopped at the same stores in town. The Cove was set up with every amenity anyone could hope for, and a few I had never thought about before coming to live there. It was nice…but sometimes I just wanted to be alone and veg.

Unfortunately, that was not going to happen today.

"So there you are," a quiet male voice said from the clearing behind me.

I shifted on the swing and answered, "Yep. Here I am. Just enjoying the peace and quiet."

He smiled. "I noticed you had vanished and wanted to make sure you were all right. It's easy to forget that all of this is new to you. It can be a bit overwhelming."

No shit, Sherlock. He was just standing there, silently, as if he was waiting for me to invite him to join me. *Did I want him to join me?* I had to admit, he was attractive. He had obviously been in the water; his blue swim trunks were wet and so was his hair. He had made some attempt to control the blonde curls by using his fingers to push them back away from his face. Other than his shorts, he was entirely bare. My eyes drifted down away from his face as I took in his muscular body, pausing for a few seconds at his abdomen to count. Not a six-pack…he was more an eight. My face grew warm when I realized he was watching me, and he knew exactly what I was doing.

The chemistry between us was palpable. The unasked question was …did either of us want to pursue the attraction? It would be hard for me to take a chance, knowing ahead of time I would be facing a lot of romantic drama and the inevitable ugliness that went along with it.

Apparently, he didn't think it a problem, because he walked over and sat beside me on the swing, while casually laying his arm along the back. I did my best to ignore the twinges of electricity I felt as his fingers grazed my shoulder. It didn't work.

Now I was faced with a choice. I didn't know much about him. Crystal said he wasn't a player and mentioned what a nice guy he was. The signs all pointed to him being a great guy. My only hesitation was did he look at me as Miss Right or Miss Right Now? Less than an hour ago he had been snuggled up close to Hannah. Of course, I had never seen him return her attention, I had just assumed he was into her. Maybe he flirted with all the girls the same way?

Knowing I was overreacting to what was possibly an innocent movement, I took a deep breath to calm my jangled nerves. If Cody was affected by my nearness, he was much better at hiding his feelings than I was. He had his head back against the swing and had closed his eyes as if he was simply enjoying the quiet.

Sounded great. Except my heart was pounding so fast in my chest I wondered how he could miss the noise. Finally, I had to break the tension.

"Won't they be looking for you?"

He chuckled. " No, I'm sure they all know where I am."

I froze. I could take that comment in two ways. I found myself wishing I could ask Crystal for advice on how to handle the situation. Either he told them he was going to find me, or they were all watching as he started up the trail. Maybe Crystal sent him to check on me!

"So, who sent you to check on me?" Crystal?"

"No one sent me. Are you always this uncertain?"

"Uncertain? What do you mean?"

"You know exactly what I mean. You feel it too."

Fuck...was I that obvious? Why did he smell so good? A warm woodsy scent with hints of rain.

"So...why did you come?"

His eyes searched mine. Instead of answering, he used his arm to turn me toward him, smiled and leaned over to kiss me.

I hesitated, then relaxed, enjoying the sensation. The kiss didn't last long, but I could not remember a previous kiss feeling like this. Sweet, like Caramel and Coca-Cola.

Almost instantly, he pulled me back into his arms, this time with passion. His tongue traced my lips, and battled my own, as the kiss deepened, pulling me farther and farther away from reality, into a world consisting of two souls and this hilltop rendezvous. Finally, he pulled his head back.

My heart was beating so fast I wondered if it was going to explode. My limbs were quivering, and it was hard to catch my breath.

"I've been wanting to do that since the day I saw you standing in the salad line."

" Oh yeah? Come to think about it, why were you in the line? You had pizza."

"It was the only excuse to get close to you, I could come up with at the moment. I had no idea you would be joining us at the table."

"Well, I'm glad you finally decided to take a chance."

He reached over, wrapping his other arm around my neck, pulling me around so that I was leaning across his lap as his lips came in for another kiss. After a few minutes, he shifted me again so that I was practically lying in the seat as he kissed me. At the end of the next kiss, we were both breathless and flushed.

"Maybe we should go join the others." His eyes reflected the passion he was doing his best to control.

"Yeah. I guess we better. I could use a cold shower right now. The lake will have to do."

I struggled to my feet, finding it harder to leave his arms than I wanted to believe. It was all I could do not to flop back down onto his lap again. I knew he was just as aroused as I was, there was no way I could miss the evidence with him in swim trunks. But it was too soon to even consider anything more than the kisses we had shared and we both knew it.

I was still tingling from his last kiss. At the memory of it, a warm glow unfurled from the pit of my belly, releasing a bit of pent-up anxiety.

It was like we were in a bubble; so easy to ignore all the chaos surrounding us, the nonessential background noise of laughter and aimless chatter made by the others as they played sharks and minnows in the water.

As we reached the beach area, I spotted Crystal approaching. Her suit was wet, she had been in the water too. She was carefully making her way across the sandy shore without shoes. Knowing how much Crystal loved pedicures, I was willing to bet the soles of her feet were baby soft. Mine was probably like shoe leather. If given a choice, I would go barefoot all the time.

Following behind her was her boyfriend Mace. The jovial senior reminded me of a ship, plowing through all obstacles, heedless of anyone reckless enough to get in his way. Trailing behind was his shadows, Dane and behind him, his twin, Danny, or maybe it was the other way around? I was still trying to keep the two boys straight. The way Mace's arm was slung across Crystal's shoulder sparked the tiniest bit of jealousy in my heart. I often wondered if I would ever find someone willing to hang with me in such an easy manner. Guilt overwhelmed me at my self-centered thoughts. Mace was my cousin, like the others and there was no doubt in my mind he was good for Crystal. That didn't change the fact that I still felt like Mace took up entirely too much of Crystals' time and attention, but under different circumstances, the places could be reversed. I realized it was a bit petty to begrudge Crystal a boyfriend just because I didn't have one. At least now, with Cody, there was a possibility. I swallowed down my bitter jealousy and smiled. I was really looking forward to a day playing in the sun.

I shimmied out of my shorts, tossing them onto the back seat of the Escalade, leaving the thin white t-shirt on since I'd forgotten to bring the wrap that matched my suit. My solid pink bikini was cut in a classical style with a halter top two sizes larger than the bottoms. My full figured curves would really stand out among the willow thing bodies around me.

It was weird, I spent almost every available moment in a swimsuit back in California but walking down the beach in California didn't make me as uncomfortable as taking that first step away from the SUV did today. I'd made it over to the blanket and dropped my t-shirt before anyone noticed. But once that shirt came off, the catcalls began.

Mace took one look and let out a long wolf whistle that immediately got the attention of all the boys. They immediately joined in, calling out lewd suggestions, offers to help me learn to swim, even one or two offers of marriage. My already ruddy skin blazed, and the Native blood became evident as my skin grew redder and redder. Only Cody resisted the urge to join in.

Crystal blushed, hearing the boys loud, raucous comments.

"Hey!" Crystal scowled and punched Mace in the arm. "Stop it." There was a brief moment of uncomfortable silence before Crystal started giggling at the shocked expression of Maces' face.

"She knows I'm just teasing her," Mace protested. "Isn't that right, Mem?"

"Oh, come on. I'm sure he didn't mean anything by it," Dane added. "It was a compliment."

Part of me really enjoyed feeling like I was the center of attention for a change. Part of that might have been the residual effects of Cody's kisses, but I was certain the bikini had something to do with it. I could see the heat in Cody's eyes as I walked across the sand to the blanket, we had spread out near the tree line.

I sank down onto the quilt and reached for my tanning butter, hoping to take advantage of the hot afternoon sun.

Cody grinned. "I can rub that on if you need a hand." An undercurrent of magnetic attraction crackled in the air and we both felt it. The idea of Cody's hands on my body made me shiver but I resisted the impulse to say yes and decided not to push my luck.

"I've got it, for now, thanks." I applied the creamy paste to both my legs, shoulders and my stomach before carefully adding a thin coat to the tops of my breasts and my face. There was a dry towel lying beside my beach bag, so I folded it to use as a makeshift pillow. The addition of sunglasses and a cold coke completed my pre sunbathing routine. For once, since arriving in the Cove, I was really content.

"You look like a cat who just finished off a bowl of cream." Crystal gave me a sideways smile. "So what have you guys been up to? Or should I ask?"

I took Crystals comments with a grain of salt. Crystal had really been upset over Michael's death, so I was happy to see Mace making her smile again. We had a lot in common. Like Crystal, I understood what it felt like to be intimate with someone one day and be gone from their life the next. There were obvious differences, Crystal lost Michael through some kind of strange accident. No one was talking about what happened, but from what little I had gleaned, it had been a particularly gruesome way to die.

My hesitation was completely different. Two

days after I'd lost my V card, I had been jerked from the group home and shuffled across the state without being able to give Jamie any contact info at all. To make it even worse, the police had confiscated my cell phone and all my contacts were inside it. I'd searched through social media and sent him a friend request on Facebook, but he hadn't accepted it. Jamie had obviously cut all ties to our past together. Since his profile now said *in a relationship*, I doubted I would ever hear from him again.

At least I hadn't been in love with him. Having my heart ripped out and stomped on would have made the move impossible. Even knowing it had nothing to do with me, had pushed me to build a thicker skin. So no one had gotten close enough to matter since Jamie.

I decided to stop berating myself. Crystal was right, I didn't need to cry over someone who didn't deserve it. He never appreciated me anyway, I was never the right one, I was just the right now. Crystal was the only one in the family who had the remotest clue about any of my secrets, especially when it came to the opposite sex, but so far, she had kept her confidences between the two of us.

"We are going to play volleyball, you want to join?" Mace pulled Crystal to her feet after she put on her tennis shoes.

I glanced toward the court, noticing Hannah was already standing by Cody and Paul.

"No. I think I'm going to lay here in the sun and veg out. You guys go ahead." I watched them until they joined the others, then I closed my eyes and dozed off in the sun.

*****

Ouch!

Startled out of my sleep by the sharp pain in my thigh, I sat up and immediately wished I hadn't moved. I was surrounded by flying insects! And they liked to bite. Make that sting. At this point in time, I didn't care what you called it. It hurt.

Lying less than three feet from my head was a large paper nest about the size of a basketball. Three more hornets stung me before I was able to organize my panic enough to realize I need to get away. I screamed and began running for the water.

Shield! The voice inside my mind was screaming something about shields but I had no idea what it meant.

I vaguely remembered reading somewhere that hornets would not follow you into the water. Despite being stung over and over I somehow managed to reach the lake and dive in. Taking a deep breath, I swan underwater as long as I could, wanting to get away from the spot where I had gone under. My body felt like it was on fire. I surfaced long enough to gasp in another breath of air and noticed there were still a few angry hornets flying overhead. So I repeated my underwater swim.

This time when I surfaced, I was no longer being followed by the angry wasps, but I was even farther away from the others. I wondered if any of them had noticed my crazy run for safety? My head was spinning, and my muscles began to cramp. I had no idea how many hornets had stung me, I only knew it was too many. I was getting sick. My throat was swelling, and it was difficult for me to breathe. I tried screaming for help, but I could not get the words out. Somehow, I managed to reach the edge of the water before everything went black.

CHAPTER 9

HOSPITAL

When I opened my eyes, it hurt; everything was white… and the light above me was very bright. In the background, I could hear a steady beep…beep...beep that was really starting to annoy me. I struggled to throw the lightweight cover off and felt a sharp sting as the needle in my arm was pulled out of position.

"What the hell…."

"She's awake!" an excited male voice rose in pitch as he called out to someone just outside the room. It sounded like Cody but why would he be in my home. Then I remembered the Hornets and the lake and put two and two together. Not home. Hospital. But how did I get to a hospital?

"Is anyone here?" The blur in my vision was gradually fading as my eyes adjusted to the artificially bright light. It was definitely a hospital room, no one in my family would ever paint a bedroom such a sickening pea green color. My aunt Peggy would never allow a metal hospital bed with side rails in their home. I have no memory of how I got here. None. The last thing I remembered was diving into the lake to escape the hornets. I wondered where all the nurses were. The last time I was in the hospital, they were everywhere. Looking around, I noticed a call button on the head of my bed and pushed it, expecting someone to answer my page. After a minute I began to get aggravated. Why wasn't anyone answering me? It's not like the boy hadn't heard me, he had called out to someone. So where were they.

I was just about to try the whiney baby voice that always seemed to get my foster parents attention when a young woman dressed in a nurse's uniform showed up. She walked over and pushed a button on the machine with the annoying beep, and it finally stopped making that annoying noise. Without saying a word to me, she glanced at her watch, made a notation on the clipboard lying on a table beside the bed, offered me a slight smiled and then left the room, placing the clipboard in a bin attached to the door on her way out.

Obviously, she had no intention of answering any questions. I could hear her talking to someone just outside the room, but I could not make out what they were saying. In frustration, I snatched the thin pillow from behind my head and tossed it out the door.

This time when the nurse entered the room, the expression on her face had changed from placid neutrality to one of shocked disapproval.

"You must be feeling better," she said as she raised my head and slipped the offending pillow back into its normal position.

"Where am I," I asked again, not that I was really expecting an answer, but figured it was worth a shot.

Just for a moment, her eyes softened. "I'll let them know you can have visitors." She left, closing the door behind her.

Still no answer to my question. California nurses were trained not to answer questions. Some hippo rule, or something like that. So I decided to give her a few minutes to send someone in before I unhooked the thingy from my arm and started looking for someone with enough authority to actually answer my questions. My head was beginning to feel like the bass drummer in the school band was warming up for a solo of Wipeout. I didn't know if I could handle the complete song.

Just as I was resigning myself to the possibility of really having to make a break for it, the door to my room opened and two familiar faces barreled toward my bed, pushing and shoving each other as they both tried to hug me at the same time. I was as excited to see Crystal and Cody as they were to see me.

The smirk on the face of the girl who entered in their wake showed she evidently didn't feel the same way. My cousin Hannah, of course.

"Whoa! Slow down. I'm glad to see you too." I was practically screaming; my body was shaking, and my hands were trembling but somewhere in the back of my mind a voice kept saying, *it's alright. They are just happy to see you.*

"Cody has been frantic," Crystal said. "They wouldn't tell us anything. And getting Hannah's mom and dad to talk about it, is almost impossible."

"Dang. I must have been out of it. I hate that I messed up your day at the lake."

"We can go to the lake anytime. How are you feeling?"

"Fine. I don't remember much…well, I don't remember anything about the helicopter flight.

They must have given me something for the pain. I don't even feel the stings anymore."

Crystal looked at Cody and he shrugged.

"This is the first time you have woke up since the hornets attacked you."

"I don't remember anything. What kind of medicine did they give me?"

The blonde boy appeared shocked by my question. "The doctors only gave you antivenom for the stings. No pain meds, just fluids to keep you hydrated."

"That sucks. How did you get here so fast? I only woke up a little while ago."

"I've been here the whole time, waiting to see if you would make it. Well, we did take turns hitting the snack machines but other than that…"

"Great. So where is here?"

"Duh…the hospital," Hannah said.

I decided right then I did not like Hannah any more away from the Cove than I did when we were at home.

"Can you be a bit more specific? Like, how long have I been here? How did I get here? Where the hell here is?

"The Lake? The hornets? Almost drowning? Nothing rings a bell?" Hannah had no problem showing her disbelief…and lack of concern.

"Don't be such a beeottch Hannah. The doctor said she might not remember much. Like PTSD or something."

I didn't remember anything after running for the lake. My memory was blank.

"Don't upset her Crystal. They said maybe her memory will come back."

"Maybe!" *I didn't like the way that sounded.*

"Calm down. What's the last thing you remember?" Cody waited for my answer.

"Waking up surrounded by bees. Being stung. Running for the water. Then things get blurry."

"I'm glad you are okay. It was touch and go for a while. I got you here as fast as I could but …." He looked at me and I realized his cheeks were wet. *Was he crying*? He moved away from the bed and stood by the window staring out at two pigeons walking along the window ledge. I was curious about what he was finding so fascinating, but the nurse came back and suddenly everyone got quiet.

"I'll think I'll go get our stuff," Hannah said. "Want a coke? Can you even have a coke? Can she," she asked the nurse.

"Sorry, I'm just here to give her an antibiotic,"

she replied. "She should wait for the doctor and ask him the questions."

"Well, I'm going back to in the waiting room," Hannah said. "I don't want to be in here when she remembers she's deathly afraid of needles. Besides, my phone needs charging and there's wi-fi in here."

I was liking Hannah less and less each moment. Did she ever think about anyone but herself?

"Just ignore Hannah, her ear would fall off if the phone wasn't holding it on," Cody said.

I decided I did like Cody. He wasn't as cute as Robert, but he was nicer. More protective. And a great kisser! Hmmm, how did I know that?

"I'm afraid of needles?" I asked Crystal.

She stared at me for a minute before she grinned and nodded. "Always have been. Or at least that's what you told me. You haven't needed to challenge that statement since you moved to Winter's Cove."

I take one look at the syringe in the nurse's hand and that was it; everything started spinning. Whether I was scared, or it was a reaction from being told I was scared, didn't matter. Either way, it was affecting me.

Cody chuckled, "Always will be." He moved back to the side of my bed and held my hand as I braced myself for the needle.

The young nurse shook her head, "It goes into your IV silly. It won't hurt at all."

"Wait!" Cody grabbed her arm just before she pushed the needle into the IV. "What' is that? It looks like the penicillin my doctor gives me."

"That's what was ordered. Penicillin."

It didn't mean a thing to me, but Cody turned bright red and lunged at the startled nurse, grabbing her by the arm before she could push the plunger.

"No!" he screamed. "Are you trying to kill her? She's allergic to Penicillin."

The nurse looked puzzled, but she quickly checked the clipboard. "It doesn't say anything about Penicillin allergies."

Cody's face grew red. "That's because her bracelet is missing. She wears it all the time. I noticed it at the lake. It was on her wrist when she arrived."

"Wait a minute. I do remember seeing a bracelet. Where is it? Somebody needs to answer a few questions. I will be right back." The young nurse was puzzled. She was certain the patient had been wearing a medical alert bracelet when she was admitted to the floor. She needed to immediately talk to her supervisor.

Suddenly I was very interested in what Cody had to say. Part of me wondered if this was really happening? I've heard of people having dreams so real they woke up screaming. This wasn't exactly a dream… this was almost a nightmare. I wasn't sure the nurse believed Cody, but at least she was worried enough about accidentally killing a teenage girl that she decided to go look for someone with more authority, my Doctor I hoped. Someone had to have ordered the penicillin. Since I wasn't sick, I had no idea why they were going to give me an antibiotic. I wanted answers … and the coke. I started rambling, saying the first thing that popped into my mind without caring how much sense it made.

"I really need a coke. Maybe two. And a Snickers bar. And some Micky D's. A Big Mac and French fries sound so good. I'm starving.

"Oh hell." Cody shut his mouth quickly and took a deep breath. I could tell he had something he wanted to tell me but needed to wait until the nurse left before he did."

Crystal looked almost as angry as Cody.

For some reason, I wasn't upset. If what Cody said was true; it meant something didn't add up. I couldn't remember much but the longer I was awake, the clearer things became. I was definitely in the Hospital. Cody's face had said yes. I could see high rise buildings out the window, so I had to be in a city. I had no memory of riding in an ambulance, but Cody had said something about him getting me here as fast as possible, so he may have driven me himself. I must have been stung by a lot of hornets. I remember reading that more than 10 would make you sick but a healthy human could stand the venom of up to 500. But why did I survive? I have a lot of allergies, and bees are one of them. My body would have gone into anaphylactic shock in minutes.

I waited impatiently for the nurse to finish up and leave. Then I pounced.

"How long have I been here?"

"Ugh…three days."

"Three days!"

"Yeah. You were really sick. They were not sure you were going to make it. If Cody hadn't …" Cody elbowed her, and she stopped talking.

"She doesn't need to know all the gruesome details."

"Okay. Start from the beginning. I was asleep on the beach. I woke up and bees were everywhere. There was a big round nest lying beside my head."

"Yeah. About that. No one knows where it came from."

"Well, it didn't just appear out of thin air!"

Neither answered so she continued.

"I remember swimming under water until I was away from the swarm. Then I started to feel sick, so I headed for the beach. I think I made it to shore but after that zilch."

"Yeah. It was a lucky accident that Coral found you. She was on her jet ski and saw you lying there. You were around the bend and out of sight of anyone at the marina."

"You looked bad. Your face and body was swollen and puffed out. If Cody didn't recognize the pink bikini, we would not have known it was you. You were turning blue because you could not breathe. We thought you would die."

But I didn't die. From what I'd been told, I should have died. Murphy was almost an hour away from the cove. Cody must have driven like a maniac to get me here.

"Well, you guys will have to put up with me a

little longer. Somebody up there must be looking out for me, but I have no idea why."

And then I heard a voice in my head……. *Because we need you.*

"Cody?" I asked hesitantly.

"Yeah. I'm here."

He was grinning like a pot belly pig with a plate of peanut butter pancakes. Now, why did I think of that? "Does the snack machine have snickers?"

"Yeah. I should have thought of that. You always have one with your coke."

"Ughhhh? Do I like pigs?" I felt like an idiot asking that one.

He broke out laughing. "Yes, you do. In fact, you have a pet pig. You bought it at the flea market last week. The man told you it was a miniature pig and wouldn't get any bigger than a poodle. He lied. She's going to get bigger than a Rottweiler. I'd say Princess will be a good 150 pounds and spoiled rotten by the time she's full grown. We've been feeding her for you but all she does is mope around. I think she misses her mommy." He pulled out his phone, searched through a few pages and then he showed me a picture of an adorable black piglet lying on a dog bed. Her furry head lay on a pink pillow and she was covered by a pink and blue plaid baby blanket that reached about halfway up her well-rounded belly.

She wasn't plump...she was a fat piggy. But she looked like she was loved. I couldn't help but giggle at the image of the two boys popping grapes into that oversized maw. My memory was coming back. Princess had very sharp teeth and two tusks hidden just inside that adorable mouth. They were lucky she hadn't taken off a finger.

My thoughts were interrupted by the return of my nurse and a pudgy middle-aged man in a white jacket with a flashlight in his pocket and a sphygmomanometer hanging around his neck. Every hair on my arm instantly stood on end. From the way the nurse deferred to him, I could only assume he was my doctor however every instinct in my body was urging me to run.

"So how are we feeling today," he asked. "I hear there was a slight mix-up in your medication. Well, no harm was done." He turned to the nurse. "Put this order in for her medication and would you please bring our young patient a coke? A little caffeine won't hurt her."

No harm was done? Penicillin would have put

me into shock…maybe even killed me and he says no harm done like it was no worse than giving me the wrong flavor of ice-cream. I waited, wondering if the little voice was going to make another comment but it chose to remain silent. Was this a sign of early insanity? Or possibly the result of trauma. Maybe I hit my head running from the hornets?

"Are you all right Memory?"

My imaginary friend may not be worried about me, but Cody was.

"No. Get me out of here. Please!" I tried to shift my body into a more defensive position on the narrow hospital bed. The side rails were up so I couldn't slide out, but I was certain I could roll forward faster than they could walk if it became necessary to make a quick escape. Cody was giving the doctor hell about the medication mix up, but the Doctor wasn't really paying much attention to his threats.

"Let me put it to you this way, if anything happens to Memory, you won't have to worry about your insurance being paid up, "he stated. "I will hunt you down no matter where you are and make you sorry you were ever a doctor."

The doctor's eyes grew cold and dark. "Young

man, you are starting to become an annoyance. Are you threatening me?"

There was something about his voice…. I could almost remember…. It was raining… and dark…. And I could hear someone talking but I couldn't see who it was…."You will never save them in time. One day you will perish just like your parents. You only live now because they do not allow me to kill you. But that day will come."

"You!" I pointed at the doctor. "You were there. You were at the hospital when my parents died."

"Don't be silly child," he smiled. "You're letting your imagination run wild. Your parents died in an auto accident."

"Then how did you know it was an auto accident?"

His expression changed. No trace of the friendly smiling doctor remained on his face. "I really wish you hadn't caught that. I slipped up. It won't happen again. Now I have a few more loose ends to clean up."

Cody appeared perplexed by our conversation but for some reason, he didn't say anything. I knew that wasn't normal, but I had no idea how I knew it. He wasn't moving either, he just standing by the door staring off into space.

You're in danger. Get out! The voice was back again! Without thinking, I launched myself into a roll down the bed straight at the doctor. We both went crashing to the floor, immediately followed by the stainless steel IV stand that was holding the bag still attached to my arm by the plastic IV lines. I tried to grab his arm, but he was extremely strong, tossing me to the side without any visible sign of effort. My head hit something hard and everything blurred out. It must have opened up a cut because blood was trickling down my forehead into my left eye making it difficult to see. And I couldn't concentrate.

Cody had finally noticed something was wrong. He made a grab for the doctor, who stomped away in a huff, mumbling under his breath about uppity teenagers.

No!!!! I struggled to rise, but I was tangled in the IV line, and every time I moved the needle jabbed into my arm. I knew it was only a matter of time before the doctor found an orderly and returned to kick Crystal and Cody out of the Hospital. There was no way I was staying there a moment longer. I reached for the IV, intending to pull it out. I must have blanked out for a second because when I looked again, Crystal was standing beside Cody and they were arguing with the doctor, giving me an opportunity to step back away from the door.

I had managed to untangle myself and pull the offending IV from my arm. There was no way I was staying there alone after the altercation. I was determined I wasn't getting back into that bed no matter what they said. Call it street smarts or gut instinct or just old fashioned stubbornness, but I was leaving that place now. First, I needed clothes, then shoes, then I was out of here.

Did I have clothes? I arrived in a pink bikini. I searched the drawers of a side table, but it was empty. So was the closet. Since I was wearing pajama's someone must have brought them… they would have to do. Pushing myself to my feet I took two steps forward then everything started spinning. I thought I heard Cody call out my name, and I begged, "please get me out of here," then everything went black…

***

I woke up in the back seat of Crystals Escalade, Cody had my head in his lap, and he was asleep. Crystal was singing along to a song by Buck Cherry. All was right in the world. I closed my eyes.

CHAPTER 10

BAD DREAMS

No! I woke up screaming, but I was not alone. Crystal was holding my hand and Cody was sitting in the chair next to my bed. My own bed. The one in my room back in the cove. I wasn't in the hospital any longer.

"How are you feeling?" Hannah was stretched out on the loveseat next to my bed doing her nails.

"I'll live." *Not that you care*. I wondered why she was here? It wasn't as if she had been interested in anything I did before now.

"Great, I tell dad you are awake." She gathered her things and waltzed out of the room. Evidently, she had been ordered to watch me until I woke up. At this moment I was ready for any excuse that would keep Hannah occupied and out of my business.

"Are you ok? I think you were having a bad dream." Cody really seemed worried.

A bad dream? It was a freaking nightmare!

She had been through it all before. It was a dream I often wished I could forget but it never seemed to happen. I could remember it as if it was just yesterday. It was after Mikki died.

I had been pleasantly surprised to discover I wasn't going to be placed into another group home. Instead, I would be living with a childless couple in an upscale suburban country club neighborhood.

I wondered how many favors Cooper had to call in to get me placed into such an isolated location? There was no way it was the luck of the draw. By isolating me from peer support, he was leaving nothing to chance, ensuring I would have no ability or reason to contact DFACS. The van driver gave his name to the guard at the gatehouse and was immediately passed through. The Holtzclaw's were expecting us.

I was still surprised when we pulled up in front of an elegant French Chalet styled brick home to see a well-dressed couple waiting for our arrival. They reminded me of the parents on the old black and white serial Ms. Paula always watched. Something about a woodchuck. Or maybe a beaver. I get them mixed up. It was an old show anyway.

The social worker said that Marsh Holtzclaw, my new foster father, was a CEO for a major corporation and spent a lot of time on the road. He was a tall, reasonably handsome man with dark brown hair and greying sideburns. Athletic and suntanned, he looked much younger than his wife.

She reminded me of so many of the women I'd seen entering the church for the weekly addiction meetings. The same dry hair, poochy stomach, and jaundiced eyes. I could smell the whiskey on her breath from five foot away.

Mr. Holtzclaw grasped my hand warmly, welcoming me into the home. He also said he hoped his wife and I would become great friends. It didn't take a genius to figure out what he really hoped was that I would keep the bipolar alcoholic housewife occupied while he was on the road, so he would not be pestered every few minutes about when he would be home again.

"Call me Diane," her new foster mother said. "I am too young to be your mother, so maybe a big sister?" She actually had a wine glass in her hand and sipped it between comments. I winced at the sour scent of her body. One of the councilors had said that was caused by liver failure and she had all the telltale signs.

"Yes, Ms. Diane," I replied, knowing that it would irritate her being called Ms. I had been a part of the system long enough to know that sugary sweet demeanor would begin to fade as soon as the departing van turned the corner of the cul-de-sac. I wondered what kind of dream world Diane lived in. Despite the Botox injections and expensive dye job, she was easily forty and like most alcoholics, she looked her age and more. My mother had been nineteen when I was born. That gave Ms. Diane a good five years grace on the "not old enough" comment. I figured if she kept drinking her liver would give out long before she accepted the idea that she looked like she could be a teenager's mother. From his expression, I figured Marsh was just counting down the days until he would be free.

"This will be your room," Diane said. "Just unpack your things and come down to the den when you are finished. Then we can talk." She sat my battered old case on the floor and left me to my own devices.

I breathed a sigh of relief as soon as the door closed behind her. The room was definitely an improvement over the group home, even though it wasn't my taste. Decorated in an extremely girly style, it could have been a spread in Better Homes and Gardens. The big four poster bed was old fashioned, but the rest was upscale and very feminine. The colors were all calming shades of pastels; tangerine, lemon yellow, and lime greens with hints of creamy beige. There was a small sitting area with two matching tub chairs and a reading lamp, an enormous mirrored dresser, and a closet easily as big as the room I had shared back in the center. The three blouses and the solitary dress I owned looked pathetic hanging in the vast emptiness. I thought about hanging the extra pair of jeans and three t-shirts I had placed in the drawers but decided it wasn't worth the effort. Then I opened the remaining door and found heaven.

My own bathroom.

In all my moves, the one thing I always hated was sharing a bathroom with a group of strangers. There was never any privacy, I rarely got to take a hot shower and shampoo seemed to vanish almost as soon as it was bought. I could suffer through almost anything if it meant being able to keep my own bathroom. The oversized soaking tub was perfect, and the shower was a separate glassed-in enclosure….with three showerheads, front and back, and an enormous rain sprinkler head in the center of the stall.

I was visibly trembling in anticipation when the knock came on the door and Ms. Diane announced dinner would be ready in ten minutes. I resigned myself to waiting and went to join my new foster family downstairs.

Dinner turned out to be Chinese Takeout. I eagerly pigged out on Happy Family, Seafood Wo-Ba, fried rice, and shrimp eggrolls. I even tried a few bites of the Hunan Beef and Kung Pow Chicken that Diane adored. Maybe things were looking up for me if this was what life in a normal family was like. After dinner I excused myself and relaxed in the soaking tub for over an hour, reading the mystery book I had borrowed from the library downstairs; then fell asleep almost immediately after crawling between the crisp white Egyptian cotton sheets.

*****

The sun had been up for some time before I woke up. Completely contented for once, I stretched, enjoying the feel of the soft cotton against my skin. The sheets at the center were always clean, but they had never felt anything like these. Someone had even added a scent to the wash, making them smell like an early morning rain shower on a freshly cut field of lilacs. Heavenly.

I was surprised to realize I was hungry. Breakfast was never one of my favorite meals. Practically dancing down the stairs after I dressed in my favorite jeans and t-shirt, I searched for something to eat.

Diane was nowhere in sight, but the kitchen was occupied by a wizened little Asian woman who ushered me to a sunny breakfast room just off the kitchen. I figured it was where the family usually took their meals.

"You must be Memory. I'm Sung, the cook, and housekeeper. Mrs. Holtzclaw won't be joining you for breakfast. Her day starts a bit later than yours did. She should be joining you for lunch, or maybe we should call it brunch."

Her not being an early riser after a night of hard drinking was unsurprising. Neither was the idea that the Holtzclaw's had a cook. The vision of Ms. Diane covered in flour in a sweltering hot kitchen kept popping into my mind, and I struggled to suppress a giggle. The woman looked like she could burn water.

Sung asked what I usually had for breakfast, shook her head at the idea of cold cereal and 2 percent milk, and disappeared back into the kitchen. In less than ten minutes she was back, carrying a tray with fresh orange juice, two crispy pancakes, link sausage, and an over medium egg. Not only was it hot; it also tasted great.

"After you eat, you might want to check out the neighborhood, or if it's too soon, you can watch TV in your room."

"There's a TV in my room?"

She laughed, a warm deep throaty guffaw that was nothing like her appearance. " I take it no one thought to show you the controller. When you finish, call me, and I will show you where everything is."

I immediately decided I loved her.
*****

Stretched out on my bed, snacking on fresh fruit while I flipped through the channels on my own 32-inch flat screen, I began to worry that everything I was experiencing was not real. That was the only scenario that would explain everything that had happened to me. I had to be passed out in the basement of the group home after drinking cheap vodka and enjoying a wonderful dream. Any time now, someone would wake me up and my life would go back to normal. Either that or I was in a coma in Charity Hospital after Cooper tried to kill me to keep me quiet. If that was the case, I'd be better off dead.

Two hours later, I had my answer. Cooper had killed me, and I was in Hell. Ms. Diane had to be the spawn of Satan. There was no other answer for the drastic personality change.

It started as soon as she got out of bed.

"Memory! Memory! I need you. Come here now." Her piercingly high pitched shriek came over the intercom as she screamed for me to join her.

Where was here? Sung had mentioned Ms. Diane always had brunch about this time of day. Maybe she was there. I didn't bother with shoes, I ran barefoot down the stairs to the breakfast room.

"We have a problem," Diane said as soon as I arrived.

I immediately went over my morning activities, trying to think of anything that might have set her off. Nothing came to mind.

"We do?" I asked quietly, hoping Diane would elaborate so I would have some idea of what I'd had done wrong, and whether it could be fixed.

"Yes. You have nothing to wear tonight."

"Tonight?" I drew a bank. Nada. No idea what she was talking about. I tried to look puzzled hoping she would have pity on me and explain what I had missed.

"Yes. Tonight. It's tonight. Go get your shoes, we have to hurry."

Since I had no idea what *it* was, but *it* was apparently something important to Diane, I hurried. That was the beginning of one of the worst days of my life.

Diane drove like a madman. We made the two-hour trip from near Malibu to Rodeo Boulevard in a little over an hour. Before it really sank in that I was inside one of *those* stores, the ones I had heard of on TV but never dared to walk inside, the clerks had stripped me down to my undies and I was trying on one horrible dress after another. Diane chose the dresses and colors.

From the little I overheard the clerks discussing I was evidently the latest in a long line of charity cases. Ms. Diane intended to milk every ounce of sympathy and social approval she could out of my presence. My opinion was neither wanted or asked. The dress Ms. Diane finally decided to purchase looked like something a fairytale princess would be wearing to a ball. The god awful Pepto-Bismol pink concoction was difficult to walk in. Sitting was even more of a nightmare. To make matters worse, my new foster mother was the chairman of the dance committee. I was to attend this dance to be seen and fawned over, and she expected me to behave as if I had just stepped out of a children's story and she was my fairy godmother. Even more disturbing, she wanted me to dance with every boy there.

After two hours of dodging sweaty teenage gropers and pimply faced Romeo's trying to shove their tongues down my throat, all I wanted was to go home.

"Ms. Diane, I'm really tired. Will we be leaving soon?" I hoped my pitiful expression might stimulate a motherly impulse. *Nope. Not a glimmer.*

"No dear, I'm head of the entertainment committee. I have to stay until the end of the party. Go dance with Morty and enjoy yourself." She pushed her toward the next adolescent nightmare. I wondered what insane scientist had injected all the member's male offspring with octopus DNA. That's was the only reasonable explanation for their behavior.

Evidentially my new foster mother had no intention of leaving until the very end.

I struggled to contain my irritation at Ms. Diane's cavalier attitude. *Did anyone present care about anything but themselves?*

As Morty tried to pull me away from the trio of giggling women, I resigned myself to several more hours of unmitigated Hell before I could return to the solitude of my new room. My head was pounding, my feet were covered in blisters and they ached in places I never knew feet could hurt. Not to mention there was an awful high-pitched buzzing coming through the speakers that was driving me crazy.

Then the strangest thing happened.

Ms. Diane was huddled with two of her cronies, possibly discussing the next torture session disguised as a cottilion. Leaving the kitchen through nearby double doors, a taller thin waiter had to sidestep to avoid a pair of wallflowers who suddenly decided to do a line dance in the center of the main walkway. There was a loud boom as both speakers exploded. He jumped and lost his balance. The tray of mixed drinks he was carrying tilted and several glasses fell over the side, splashing across the three women just as one struck her lighter to smoke a cigarette. There was an instant flash of bright light and then one of the women screamed.

Chaos erupted as it became apparent two of the women's hair was on fire. Several men pulled their jackets and used them to douse the flames, but the damage was done. The automatic sprinklers were pouring water on everything.

I stood in shock staring at what remained of my foster mother's curly red hair and the streaks of black ash running down her face. Everyone was staring at me. That's when I realized I had been laughing hysterically.

Both women were crying and the man who had spilled the drink was fired. The band blamed the ballroom on the destruction of their speakers. And no one had any idea what to do about the burn victims. Luckily someone had thought to call the fire department. Once the paramedics had arrived and transported the two victims to the hospital, they turned off the water and everyone left for home.

That's when I realized I had no idea where I was., no idea how to get to my new home, and I didn't have a key to get in when I got there.

No one was interested in taking responsibility, so DFACS was called and I was shuttled off to a juvenile holding cell, to spend what was left of the night on a wooden bench in the now filthy pink chiffon gown.

I never saw Ms. Diane again. My battered suitcase arrived with the DFACS caseworker and I was placed with Ms. Tolbert the next day.

CHAPTER 11

HORSING AROUND

I wiped the sweat from my palms once again, and slid from the passenger seat of the SUV, doing my best to appear nonchalant about the idea of climbing onto the four-legged behemoth I had promised to ride.

When Crystal had mentioned going riding to me earlier in the week, I'd answered yes without considering she might actually expect me to do it. At the time I was floating on an adrenaline high brought on by all the attention I was receiving at my first real dance. Not that I had told anyone I had never had a chance to attend a dance before.

Every year the Winters family put on an annual end of school dance at the arena, just inside the Cove grounds. While there, Crystal had taken me into the stables so I could see her favorite horse Cochise and feed him a couple of sugar cubes. The first thing I noticed when we entered the stable area was that it did not stink. I wasn't sure why I had convinced myself that horses smelled bad, but the odor was actually pleasant, a warm earthy scent that reminded me of freshly brewed beer and a field of grass that had just been mowed.

"I love riding. Why don't you come with me sometime?"

"I don't know... I haven't been on anything bigger than a Shetland pony, but if you think I will be okay?"

"It's fine. You don't have to come with me if you don't want to." Despite the casual words, I had been around Crystal long enough to recognize the tone of her voice was more of a plea than a release.

"No, I want to. It sounds like fun."

The thought of making up an excuse to stay behind crossed my mind, but I realized I was actually looking forward to trying something new.

"You're sure?"

"Yes. I'm sure."

"Great! Wear something comfortable, Jeans and boots. I'll pick you up in the morning."

She sounded happier than I ever remembered hearing her sound. It crossed my mind that she might have missed riding with Michael since she had mentioned it was something they enjoyed doing together. A niggling little fear at the back of my mind taunted me with the idea that he might have died from a riding accident but somehow, I couldn't imagine that being gruesome enough to raise a wall of silence about his death.

We hadn't stayed in the barn area long, but it was long enough for me to agree to try something I would have never attempted on my own.

I now realized I was not prepared to face my demon up close. Crystal was not going to let me out of my agreement, so I was doing my best to hide the fact that I was scared shitless. I took a deep breath and followed her into the main barn.

The central building was extremely large, with oversized box stalls running the length of each outside wall. Once we were inside, I realized there were actually four rolls of stalls, two along the center aisle and one on each side. Between the stall areas was a narrow strip of rooms, each about the size of a walk-in closet, where all the tack was stored. The back walls of the tack storage rooms formed the back walls of the central stalls. It was an amazingly organized setup. Inside the individual tack rooms was a rack to hold the saddle and blanket pad, a couple of hooks holding a bridle with the horse's name etched into a narrow brass plate, and a couple of nylon halters. There was also a small shelving unit that held various brushes and cleaning equipment, an assortment of sprays and creams that I had no idea of the use, and a small locked cabinet. I must have looked curious about the locked cabinet because Crystal told me it held prescriptions for the horse, and some of them were toxic to humans.

My mind immediately jumped to Special K, and how many of my friends back in California had messed up their mind experimenting with it. One boy's head was so muddled he walked off the edge of a five-story building. The sad part was that he had lived; if you call being in a coma and needing a machine to breathe living. Anything strong enough to tranquilize a fourteen hundred pound animal would totally overwhelm a human's nervous system. Not that Ketamine wasn't a useful drug, a lot of surgeons swore by it because it would deaden the pain receptors without shutting down the respiratory system.

Martin, the man who took care of the horses was a stickler about safety, so he kept the keys to all the cases. They only other spare was on the veterinarian's keychain. Not because of the family, but because it was a tempting target to outsiders.

Crystal had convinced me to try riding on one of the older horses in the stable. According to her, Red Robin was a fifteen-year-old chestnut gelding with the best disposition of any animal in the stable. All I knew was…he was really big…and tall. So tall I was going to need a step stool to get on him. I wondered if they had parachutes available?

Red Robin's stall was only two down from Cochise, so she would be saddling her horse while I took care of Robin. I kept glancing at Martin, hoping he might offer to help, but the old man considered the tack up process a good learning experience. He did show me how to brush his coat and that wasn't too bad. I think Robin must have liked it because his eyes closed, and he pressed his body toward the brush. He didn't even mind when I brushed his legs and feet. Martin must have sorry for me when it came time to check the bottom of his feet because he came over and lifted the hoof so I could examine it. I just nodded as he told me what to look for because I had absolutely no idea what the hell he was talking about.

Crystal passed me a woven leather lead to clip to the halter, so I could lead Robin out of his box. I was surprised by how clean the stalls were. Martin said either he or his son Jose, made it a point to clean the shavings at least once an hour during the day. He showed me the oversized pitchfork he used. It had a lot more times than a normal one, more like a rake. Each stall had about a foot of really thin shavings like you would see in a hamster cage for the horses to walk on. That surprised me.

"Doesn't it hurt their feet?"

"No. It's really thin and it flexes under their feet. Our stalls are top of the line. Underneath the shavings, there is a thick rubber pad that runs from side to side. It's perforated with tiny drain holes that allow any liquid to pass through to the sand beneath it. The sand lies atop a bed of gravel that drains into the sewer system. So their stalls never have standing water inside."

I noticed they had automatic floats in the water trough that kept them filled with fresh water at all times. They even had a screened-in paddock to walk around in that kept the flies at bay. The horses lived better than I did back in the group home. We were lucky to have a screen on the window and the only way our bedding got cleaned, was if we took the time to wash and dry them ourselves.

Red Robin suddenly looked at me and vigorously shook his head. Then he blew air across his lips making a funny sound. I immediately stepped back, my foot landing in the only unclean spot in the entire stall. It was an omen. I should have worn the boots. Now my favorite tennis shoes were trashed.

"Are you sure I will be able to handle this? He looks awfully big to me. Maybe I should just watch you ride."

"Don't be silly. Robin is an extremely well-mannered horse. My mother uses him when she rides with my father and she is scared to death of most horses. He is so easy going a gun could go off right beside him and he would not flinch. I know because Tony tested him one year. The other horses went crazy, but Robin just stood there."

I wasn't convinced. The beast was giving me the evil eye. I was certain he was waiting for me to relax and then he was going to roll on me or something equally disgusting. He already tried to pee on me when I was placing the heavy western saddle on his back. How was I supposed to know the pad had slipped down? It's not like I saddled a horse every day.

I had been on a horse once before…well, it was a pony and all it did was walk in a circle around a ring. And there was a handler there to make sure I didn't fall off. But I remember it was a really long way to the ground. I was certain I was going to fall off and get stomped before anyone noticed. It didn't happen, but I remember that pony had the same malicious gleam in its eyes.

***

Crystal eyes sparkled as her cousin edged closer to the placid gelding, acting as if she expected him to rear up and breathe fire at any moment. She did her best not to laugh as Memory struggled with the unwieldy western saddle. It was heavy cowhide over a wooden frame and probably weighed forty pounds. To make matters worse, Robin was a quarter horse, standing over 16 hands high and weighing about 1400 pounds. It had taken her months to learn how to swing the heavy saddle up onto the withers and slide it back into position. She was five-eight, an inch taller than Memory, too. That had to make it harder to do.

She was waiting for Memory to realize she

still had to get the bit into the horse's mouth. Robin was an easy bridler, unlike Cochise, the horse she was riding today. He liked to nip. If she had not been wearing her high school ring, the first time she tried putting the bit in his mouth, she could have lost a finger. Old Robin would never do that, but it was going to be hilarious watching her cousin trying to get the mouth open without touching the horse. Or getting stepped on while she was standing beside him. He did like to move around while being saddled. And he loved the blowfish trick. It was going to be hilarious.

***

Why didn't I make up some kind of excuse? After four tries I finally succeeded in settling the saddle into the right place on the horse's withers. Now I had to remember the complicated way in which the girth went on. I must have watched Crystal do the saddle knot ten times. But so far, every time I did it, it was wrong. Finally, just when I was ready to forget the entire matter and go back home, I managed to get the knot right. But she stopped me before I could get on the horse.

"Slap him on his belly before you pull the strap tight."

"Slap him? Are you trying to get me killed?" When I closed my eyes, I could picture one of those iron clad hoofs landing on my chest or stomach; even if I survived, I would be scared for life.

"No silly, it makes him blow out the air he's holding. Robin is a clown. If you tried to get on him now, the saddle would slide down when you put your weight on it."

I looked under his body, noticing he was extremely well endowed. My face flamed red and I could feel my skin tightening as I fought down the urge to make some kind of smart ass wise-crack about finally understanding the 'hung like a horse' comment. Despite what Crystal said, I was certain the beast was watching me, ready to attack as soon as I swung my hand in the direction of his privates. With my luck, I would hit the wrong target. I doubt he would think it was a funny mistake.

Crystal took pity on me and slapped his belly. Robin huffed out a long breath and she drew the strap tight before he could inhale again. That's when she handed me the bridle. I had forgotten about that little detail.

Grasping the bit firmly by the twin rings, I

stood in front of Robin, gathering my courage to attempt the insertion. It did not matter how many times she told me the beast only ate plants, those were some of the biggest teeth I had ever seen. She was crazy as hell if she thought I was going to put my hand that close to his mouth. There had to be another way. Maybe I could use the lead strap and the halter. She said he was easy going.

"He won't mind. He's had a bit in his mouth a hundred times, maybe more. It doesn't hunt, there's a gap behind his front teeth and the bit sits there in front of his back teeth. Just hold the bit by the ring on its side, and press it into his mouth, he will open up for it."

Crystal had lost her mind. The beast was looking at me like I was some kind of pesky insect he was getting ready to stomp into the ground, and she expected me to stick a cold metal bar in his mouth. I could close my eyes and visualize exactly what he was thinking, and it wasn't a pretty picture. I took a deep breath and pushed the bit into his mouth with no trouble at all. He didn't even appear to be bothered by my lack of technique. I exhaled the breath I'd been holding and smiled.

Robin followed Cochise out to the mounting block as if it was no big deal. Crystal stood by him as I swung into the saddle and waited as Martin adjusted the stirrups to my leg length, before swinging aboard her horse. Cochise was eager to be off, so Crystal had to keep a tight hold on the reins, but Robin seemed bored by his frantic prancing. He walked placidly along behind the younger horse, ignoring the geldings hints to increase his speed as though he understood how frightened I was.

After a few minutes, my body adjusted to the rhythm of his movements and I began to relax. I even let go of the saddle horn, once I managed to release the death grip. My fingers had intertwined into a contorted knot and refused to let go.

Crystal was ecstatic to see me let go of the horn.

"See, I told you it isn't scary. You just have to calm down and enjoy the ride."

She led the way off the main trail, picking a path that ran between two old oaks and across a meadow of emerald green clover. Robin snatched up a mouth or two along the way, but he kept walking the entire time. If Crystal noticed his snacking she never commented, so I figured it was okay. The path meandered along the edge of the meadow, allowing me a clear view of the various herds of cattle scattered throughout the pastures.

"Are you sure this is the right way? The path is getting pretty narrow," I asked as we left the clearing that was otherwise surrounded by dense growth and some really tall pine trees.

Crystal laughed and clucked to Cochise who eagerly sped up from a walk into a jarring trot.

I did my best not to panic as Robins' speed increased, praying my white-knuckled grip on the saddle horn would be enough as we bumped along behind them down the narrow dirt path. I quickly grew to appreciate the stirrups once I realized by putting weight on my feet, I could prevent the hard slaps against the saddle.

We had ridden about a quarter of a mile along the path when we spotted a trio of four wheelers heading our way. I immediately began to get nervous, unsure of how the horses would react when the noisy machines drew near. Even from a distance, the sound grated on my ears. I could imagine how loud it must seem to the animals.

As the trio grew closer, I could see it was the last three people I wanted to run into. Hannah and the twins. It was a shame too, most of the time the twins were all right. They liked to joke around but were never intentionally cruel. But add Hannah to the mix, and their entire personality changed. It was never obvious, but they went out of their way to pull mean little tricks, almost snipe attacks as if they were trying to impress my cousin in some way. Like now, there was no reason for them to rev their motors or sling gravel around while approaching the horses. But Hannah was doing it, so her minions followed suit.

The twins shot each other amused looks and smirked as Cochise began crow hopping around, giving little bucks and generally making it clear he did not like the noisy machines at all.

"Why are you being such a bitch? You know how he gets when you ride right up on him." She swung down off the horse, holding his halter tightly.

Crystal did not seem hesitant about tearing into Hannah, but I knew there could come a time when I might need my cousins to help, so I didn't want to do anything to further antagonize her. Besides, Robin was behaving like a perfect gentleman, and I didn't want to become the target of her twisted sense of humor.

"Fine," Hannah snapped, backing away from

the agitated gelding. But she made no effort to quiet the motors. "But you might want to take a look at his right front hoof. I think he's lost a nail."

"Damn, your right. Turn those stupid bikes off so I can check."

Amazingly, the boys listened, cutting the motors immediately. Hannah didn't turn her's off, but she did back off about fifty feet so that he would calm down. Sure enough, the iron shoe had lost a nail, and one was broken, so there was only one nail holding it onto his foot.

"Looks like I am going to have to walk him back. Come on Memory, it's going to be dark by the time we get back."

I thumped my heels against Robins side to get him to start walking and he took a couple of steps.

Then things went crazy.

First, he gave a sharp scream, and then he bolted, heading down the path at a dead run. I tried to pull back on the reins, but the maddened beast had the bit in his teeth and ignored my frantic screams. Overcome by fear, I dropped the reins and locked my fingers in a death grip around the saddle horn. The horse was running as fast as he could back up the narrow trail.

Suddenly Robin changed direction, cutting off the trail we were following at an angle, then galloping across a cattle field, sending the cows into a panic.

My voice was beginning to crack from screaming 'whoa' and 'help'. I was worried that if I lost my voice, I would be unable to call for help if anyone got close enough to me to hear. I had no idea where I was, the trail Robin was running down split several times and he seemingly chose his direction on impulse. Several times I came close to being knocked off by low limbs when he made a course correction at the last moment and used a shortcut through the woods.

Reaching a different meadow he galloped along without showing any sign of slowing his pace. Somehow, I had managed to adjust to the rhythm of his run, so I was no longer afraid of falling. Instead, I was beginning to worry about finding my way back to the barn. I prayed that was where he was going, but since I wasn't very religious, I didn't really expect it to help. Without reins, I had no way of directing him and would not know where to point him, if I did.

I turned my head, trying to spot anything that

looked familiar with no luck. Winters cove was several thousand acres and I had not seen more than five or six at the most.

Nor did I expect any help from my cousins. I listened but could not hear the sound of a four-wheeler motor. Cochise could not be ridden, so there was no way for Crystal to follow. I gave up and concentrated on staying on top of the maddened horse.

Robin was heavily lathered in sweat and his mane was tangled with broken twigs. His breath now wheezed in and out like rusty bellows. There was no way he could keep up this speed much longer.

The golden brown eyes that I had earlier found evil were now blood red and ringed with yellow. I would never consider those beautiful eyes wicked again. I began a silent chant.

Whoa. Whoa. Please stop. Whoa, Robin. Please just stop.

Without warning, he suddenly dug in his heels and slid to a stop. My body kept going, flying over his head and onto the hard ground. The sharp pain in my right wrist was the last thing I remembered as I bounced and then rolled over the edge. I was dimly aware of my body rolling and bouncing from tree to rock down the steep slope, unable to stop until I slammed into a larger rock somewhere along the bottom of the ravine. I felt a burst of intense pain as my head slammed against the stone, followed by a brief period of dizziness before I lost consciousness.

CHAPTER 12

LOST

Jose dropped the hay fork and ran. "Papa! Papa! Something's wrong with Red Robin! Look. Look!"

Martin ran from the barn, looking across the field at the old chestnut gelding galloping towards them. The elderly horses' burnished red coat was dark and lathered, soaking wet from sweat. His breathing was labored, and his eyes were rolling wildly. He stumbled, going down on one knee, then struggled back to his feet, returning to a frantic gallop as he raced towards his stall. The saddle had slid sideways, hanging awkwardly from the girth strap, while one stirrup scraped across the ground, bouncing up to strike his leg every few strides. There was no sign of his saddle pad. Or his rider. He raced toward the stable with no sign of slowing his charge.

"Move boy! He's going for his stall. Don't get

in his way!"

Jose managed to jump out the way just before the crazed quarter horse breached the entrance, still at a dead run. Robin made it three more strides before he screamed like a child and collapsed.

Martin ran to his side, but it was obvious the old fellow was dead. Martin shook his head. Something was seriously wrong. He pulled his cell and hit the speed dial button for Hugo Winters.

***

"Hello." Thank heavens he answered. Martin had been afraid he was in a meeting, or out of town

"We got a serious problem here at the stable. You need to come quick."

"I'm on my way." Hugo hung up and turned to address the men at the table. "We're going to have to continue this discussion later. There's something seriously wrong at the stables. Nick, you might want to come too. In ten years, Martin has never called for help. Hell, he has never called for any reason. It's got to be bad."

"I'll come too. Crystal was going riding today. She had Memory with her." Matias texted

Peggy to let her know he would be late. "You go on ahead. We will be right behind you."

***

Martin was examining the carcass when Hugo entered the stable. He was puzzled at how quickly he'd arrived but after working in the cove ten years, very little surprised him anymore. He waved his boss over and quickly described what had happened.

"Robin was crazed by pain when he arrived. I've never seen an animal act like that. Look at his knees. He must have fallen four or five times to tear them up like that. But that's not why I called you. He came back alone. I have no idea where the girls are."

"Call the Vet, get him out here now. I want to know what made him go crazy like that. I'll get help to look for the girls." He pulled his cell phone and started calling. He was still on the phone when Nick and Matias arrived. He quickly briefed them on the details. "Take the barn ATV's and head out toward the back pastures. Crystal loves to ride toward the falls. I will check out by the orchards. Most of the kids are at the lake but watch for the twins and Hannah, they are out there somewhere. Nick, can you try and reach someone at the lake. We need all the help we can get. There's no way Crystal would have let that horse run away like that unless there was no way she could prevent it. And that scares me."

Martin and Jose helped Nick and Matias push the ATV's out of the storage lockers, topped off the fuel and passed each one a medical kit just in case. He watched them until they passed out of sight before returning to the barn. He noticed Mr. Hugo was already gone but didn't think much about it. It totally slipped his mind as the Bell rang twice, signally someone had just passed through the main gate. Doc Wells must have been in the area too.

***

Ughhhh...

I was lying in mud at the edge of the creek when I woke up. I could taste the salt from the blood trickling down my cheek from a cut in my forehead just above my left eyebrow. My shirt was soaked, my jeans muddy and torn. I must have hit my knee on a rock as I tumbled down the hill. My knee felt like someone had jabbed a hot poker into the side, but at least I could move it. That was good because my right wrist was swollen and there was no way I could put any weight on it. I hoped it wasn't broken but it looked bad. It hurt worse than my head, and that surprised me.

Bracing my good wrist against a handy rock, I struggled to my knees and then made a three-legged crawl away from the water onto drier land. Even crawling for that short a distance left me winded. My heart pounded in my chest, my lungs struggled for air like I had asthma and my muscles were trembling. There was no way I could make it up that hill to the top of the ravine.

"Help!" I shouted, hoping someone was looking for me and close enough to hear my calls. Fifteen minutes later my voice was hoarse, and I was no closer to getting help than I was before I began shouting. The only way I was getting out was on my own two feet. Overcome by self-recrimination I rolled onto my back and stared up at the sky. There was a hawk circling above me, probably looking for his dinner. At first, I had thought it was a buzzard, but when I moved, it didn't leave, so that ruled out a scavenger. I could see the tops of a pine stand beyond the edge of the ravine. I hadn't really been able to pay much attention to the scenery while we were galloping madly through the woods. I was too busy ducking low hanging branches while maintaining my death grip on the saddle horn.

It was possible I had been in the area before, but nothing looked familiar. For all I knew, there could be several houses just beyond the wood line, but from where I was laying, there were no landmarks in sight to help me find my way back to the stable. I could tell from the location of the sun in the sky, it was late afternoon. Dark fell quickly in the mountains, it would be almost impossible to see within an hour or two at the most. My best chance of finding my way back to civilization was to continue following the creek downstream until it reached the lake. Surely, I could find help there.

The only drawback to that idea was the untamed inhabitants of the valley. My uncle Matias had warned me not to stray too far from the busier areas while exploring, citing the bears, snakes and larger predatory wildcats that inhabited the woods. He also mentioned that several packs of coyotes had been spotted. The wild dogs would not normally bother a human. Unfortunately, I was bleeding and injured, making me a tantalizing tidbit for any meat-eating predator. I heard a rustle in the underbrush along the top of the ravine and carefully studied the area, hoping to identify what had disturbed the heavy growth, but there were no further hints of movement. Not that it made me feel any safer, very few animals warned you before they attacked.

"Hello. I'm here. Help!" No response…again. *Well*, the little voice in my mind said, *you better get moving or you will be spending the night alone beside the main source of water in the area.* I decided the voice was a smart ass too.

I wished I was superstitious. When I turned my head, I spotted a perfect four-leaf clover less than a foot from where my head lay. I decided to pull it and tote it with me, figuring it couldn't hurt. For the longest time, I had carried a rabbit's foot around. Until one of the kids in the group home pointed out it hadn't been very lucky for the rabbit.

For once I listened to my subconscious mind without arguing. Using a nearby sapling for leverage, I somehow managed to struggle to my feet. My knee was not going to hold out for long. It hurt like a mutha and was already stiffening up. It was bad, there was already a golf ball sized area puffed out and full of fluid. I figured it was sprained or maybe a torn ligament, but I didn't think it was broken.

My first big mistake was feeling overconfident and forgetting about my wrist. When I accidentally bent it while attempting to stand, an intense wave of pain washed over me. I felt my vision going black and I fought to remain upright. Sweat popped out on my forehead, and I dry heaved a few times, before falling back to my knees.

Once I grew steady again, I decide to splint it. It irked me to rip up one of my favorite tees, but there was no way I could handle another burst of pain like that. There was plenty of windfall lying around the dry area beside the creek bed. Most of it was water rotted and too soft to use, but it wasn't too difficult to find three pieces short enough to use as makeshift splints. Strips from my tee wrapped tightly around the twigs would prevent me from bending it and offer some protection from accidental bumps. It wasn't the easiest thing I'd ever done with one hand, but I remembered one of my girl scout leaders tricks of using a stick to twist the ends together and it worked.

Well, now that I was on my feet and reasonably stable, what was I going to do next? No one knew where I was, and the cove was enormous. It could be days before this section of the ravine was searched, it ever. Logically, they would be looking for me near the woods where I'd disappeared from Crystal's sight or in the area where Robin is located, providing he finally decided to stop running and rest. The obvious question is upstream or down? I knew that if I followed the stream, it should join the lake somewhere downstream. I had absolutely no idea where it would lead me if I went upstream. So heading downstream is a no brainer.

Crossing my heart like I was a Catholic at prayer and offering a brief request for help to anyone up there willing to listen, I began making my way along the overgrown game path that edged the stream.

***

Hugo arrived at the orchard without spotting any sign of Crystal or Memory. He walked up a slight rise and looked out across the main pastures. There were cattle everywhere but no sign of the much taller Cochise. If the girls had been there, they were long gone by now. He decided to take the main trail back toward the barn, hoping to run across some sign that they had been in the area earlier in the day. Crystal knew this part of the cove better than anyone. If there was a reason to reach help, she knew which house was closest to her location and the best way to reach it. Nicks house was only a half mile beyond the orchard; if anything had happened in this area, she would have headed that way. Since no one had contacted him, he had to assume the girls had no way of reaching anyone. Nor had anyone located them or he would have heard from one of the searchers. It was times like this he wished there was a tracker in the family.

***

I slid down onto my ass for the forty-seventh time while attempting to cross from one side of the creek to the other. The path along the side I had been following had gradually narrowed as the wall of the ravine closed in, until it finally ended at a wide, mud and moss-covered shallows, before continuing along the other side. Against the darkening sky, the last sliver of sunlight projected enough of a shadow for me to miss seeing the loose grey rock that shifted as my foot came down atop it. At least I hadn't landed in the water this time. My most comfortable pair of jeans were now streaked with red clay, green grass stains and some kind of blackish grey slime that grew near the edge of the stream. My tennis shoes would need to be burnt. What little remained of my t-shirt did almost nothing to protect my shoulders and breasts from twigs and briars along the way. I looked terrible and felt worse.

Once I reached the other side of the creek, I was happy to discover the trail had widened once again, making its way along a sandy stretch of reasonably flat land bordered by tufts of saw-grass and scrub. It probably flooded during the rainy season but was solid at this time of the year. Further on I could see taller trees, similar to the pines I'd seen growing near to the lake shore. Even better, somewhere in the distance, I could hear the sound of a motor!

I started walking, grateful for the flat surface. There was no way I would reach the lake before full darkness, it was already becoming difficult to see, but there was a good chance the moon would be bright enough for me to continue down the trail, albeit very carefully.

As darkness closed in around me the moon rose, and the stars came out, shining brightly. Gradually my eyes adjusted to the meager light and I felt confident enough to continue onward.

The sound of a motor could no longer be heard in the distance, but that was to be expected. Most people stayed on shore after dark.

I was really beginning to feel hungry but at least there was no lack of fresh water, even though I was probably going to pay for drinking it unfiltered in a few hours. Hopefully, I would come out somewhere close to the marina. Even if no one was around, there was a phone in the main office and everyone in the family knew the door code.

About fifteen minutes later I spotted the bridge.

***

"There's two of the kids." Nick turned his ATV toward the distant pair of four-wheelers, followed by Mattias on the smaller four-wheeler. Seconds later they were pulling up beside the worn out teenagers

"Are we glad to see you. We ran out of gas over an hour ago." Hannah gave her father a hug and smiled at Nick.

"We're glad to see you too," her father replied." How did you run out of gas?"

Hannah glanced at Dane who had the decency to look ashamed.

"It was the strangest thing. We spotted Crystal and Memory on the horses and decided to annoy them a little. You know how Cochise hates it when someone revs their motor near him. We didn't get very close and only did it for a minute."

Dane didn't like talking to the old folks, especially when he knew he was about to get chewed. But he knew Hannah would gloss over the truth to keep from getting in trouble. He took over the story.

"Somehow Cochise threw a shoe. Crystal got off to check it and realized there was no way she could ride him back with the shoe hanging on by one nail."

"So the girls are walking back?" Nick asked Dane.

"No. That's where the weird part starts. All three motors were turned off and we were just standing by the bikes talking to Crystal when all of a sudden old Robin bolted. Memory was screaming for help, and by the time we got the ATV's started and took off after her, she had disappeared." He looked puzzled. "I didn't think that old horse could run like that. He lit out like his tail was on fire, up the main trail until they reached the split, then he cut off onto a game trail that led into the woods."

Dane had the decency to look ashamed. He could tell by the scowls on the two men's faces that neither liked hearing what he was saying.

"We finally got the dang things cranked and took off following the old trail through the woods. Danny stayed to keep Crystal company while we searched, figuring from the way Robin was acting, Memory would either fall off or get scraped off by a limb. But we never spotted her or the horse. We were heading back to the main trail when Hannah ran out of gas. I still have a little, but we filled up at the same time. I doubted it would be enough to get back to the barn and I didn't want to leave Hannah alone."

"Yeah," Hannah said. "Memory is probably pigging out in front of the TV while we get ate up by mosquitos---" She stopped talking when she saw the anger flash in her father's eyes. He didn't like hearing what she was saying.

"Robin is at the barn. He's dead. There's no sign of Memory." Mattias pulled out his cell, checked for signal and scowled. " No signal. I'm going to need to get higher to reach Hugo. Maybe he's found some sign of Memory. Nick has a can of gas. Take enough to get back to the barn and let them know we are still searching. "

Neither teen opened their mouth.

***

There was a well-worn access trail up to the bridge. It took me a while to climb up with only one hand and a stiff knee, but I was ecstatic to finally reach the road. I was even happier to see a signpost that mentioned a public campground straight ahead. Evidently, I was no longer on Winters property. Most of the lake was public access so even though it was the middle of the week, there was a good possibility someone would be camping in one of the rental spaces. The motor sound had come from the campgrounds. I started hobbling in that direction.

I came across the first camping space about fifteen minutes later. It was empty. Thru the trees, I could see the moon reflecting off the lake nearby. The sound of the water lapping against the shore was strangely calming. The sight of an old picnic table sitting beside a battered metal grill reminded me of how tired I was. When I got closer, I could see that the benches were gone but the top was still there, so I backed up against it and lay back, then squirmed until most of my body was on top. Surely by now, someone had realized I was missing and begun a search. Maybe I should remain there until daybreak and then look for help?

I was just about to doze off when I heard the faint sounds of a man singing and the strain of an acoustic guitar. Freezing in place, I listened, and could almost make out the direction when the sounds ended abruptly.

"Damn!" There was no way I was going to stay on that table when there were people camped somewhere nearby. It only took a minute to slide off the table and find my balance again. Gritting my teeth because my knee had tightened up while I rested, I hobbled back to the main road and started walking toward the next campsite. It was empty too.

Two sites further I spotted a fire somewhere farther down the road. By concentrating on the fire I was able to hear the faint sounds of a woman singing to a guitar. It wasn't the strong male baritone I heard earlier, but hearing a female voice made me more comfortable about barging into their campsite. I had made it about five hundred feet when the music stopped, and I heard the sound of a boat motor starting.

"Help" I screamed. "Don't leave, please. I

need help." There was no answer. I began moving as fast as I could in that direction, forcing my body into a strange shuffle, hop, hobble, hop pattern to keep the weight off my bad knee as much as possible. The fire was out but I could smell the smoldering wood long before I reached the campsite. It was empty, they were gone.

***

Hugo was furious. Everyone was out searching for Memory, but after seven hours of searching, there was still no sign of her. Despite his aversion to allowing outsiders onto the property, he had agreed to allow the sheriff's department to bring in tracking dogs in hopes of locating her. The dogs were given her scent and they took off, but so far, they had not been able to locate any possible clues to her disappearance. It was as if she had vanished.

The veterinarian's report had not helped matters. Martin had used a small forklift to flip Robin onto his opposite side. There was an extremely large swelling on his left flank, one that had not been made by natural means. Doc Haynes was certain someone had hit the elderly horse with a dart, injecting some manner of irritant into the normally docile animal. He had withdrawn a sample of the tissue to have it analyzed and identified, but it was evident someone had intentionally caused the old gelding death.

The question was why? Obviously, the target wasn't Robin, no one would have a reason to hurt the horse. So someone was out to get Memory and perhaps they had succeeded. He had a good idea about why she had been targeted but had no idea who had pulled the trigger on the dart gun.

He sighed, he'd hoped to have at least a week to prepare before having to address this situation. Losing his son Michael last month had left a raw ache that refused to release its hold on his heart. Now he would have to fight thru his grief and take charge once again. Would it ever stop?

Daylight was only a couple of hours away. They had a helicopter in the air now, using heat thermography to search the less habitable areas of the cove without any results. Either she wasn't on the grounds, or her body temperature had dropped below 90 degrees. Neither was an option he wanted to consider.

Nick knocked on the office door and passed him a cup of hot coffee and a couple of donuts. Matias followed him into the room and shut the door behind him. Both men took a seat. It was time to talk about what ifs…They had just begun to talk when the phone rang.

CHAPTER 13

BARBEQUE

My stomach rolled uncomfortably as I slid into the car with Crystal. I wanted nothing more than to duck out of the cookout at Tony's house, but I knew I was expected and if I didn't show up, everyone would be looking for me. A week had passed since my riding accident, and I was feeling fine. Other than the cast on my wrist, it was as if nothing had happened. My hesitation to attend the party had nothing to do with that. I simply did not like meeting new people.

By now everyone knew about the attempt on my life by people or parties unknown. I had walked along the park road for about a mile before discovering a twenty-four-hour bait shop and convenience store at the intersection of the park entrance and one of the older highways.

After opening the door, I approached the cashier station, and announced," My name is Memory Winters, I'm hurt. Help me please." A wave of dizziness swept over me and things grew dim, and then black.

I woke up in the back of an ambulance on the way to the local medical center.

"Well hello," the paramedic said. "How are you feeling?"

"Like I've been thrown from a horse, rolled down a ravine and then walked for hours on a fucked up knee." As usual, my smart ass attitude was there to support me. Surprisingly, my sarcastic remark did not upset her. In fact, she made a joke.

"So we will need to get an x-ray of your knee and your wrist in addition to your head. Is anything else not working?"

"Yes. But I ache in so many places I can't pinpoint the exact location."

"Well, that's to be expected after an accident. I will suggest the doctor do a full series of tests to make sure we don't miss anything. I can't give you anything for pain, but we will be at the hospital soon. Just try and relax."

She scribbled a few things on a clipboard and then checked to make sure my I.V. was flowing correctly.

My Uncle Matt and Hugo were both at the

hospital when I arrived. They were upset about what happened but cautioned me about discussing it within range of the hospital employees. I was curious about the secrecy but figured they knew best. The Doctor came in to talk to us after the x-rays, CT and MRI were complete. She explained that I had been given fluids to replace the ones I had lost, that I had a minor concussion and a possible broken wrist. Three hours later I was released with instructions to stay in bed and keep the cast on my wrist for three weeks. That screwed up my time at the lake, but it could have been much worse.

My family was probably beginning to think I was something of a clutz; this was the second time I'd been to the Hospital in less than a month.

I heard rumors that Robin had been bitten by a snake and that was why he took off the way he did but no one wanted to talk about it, so I let it go. But doubts remained…something didn't add up. It seemed to me that if a snake big enough to kill a horse was slithering around on the ground when the horse went crazy, one of the others would have noticed it.

***

As Crystal approached the massive circular

drive that surrounded Uncle Nicks home, I found myself wishing once again that I had my own car. After getting my learner's permit in California, I had saved all year and had been proud of the eleven hundred dollars I had put away. Now I realized eleven hundred dollars would not buy a decent set of tires, much less a good quality automobile. Crystal drove a Cadillac Escalade, with heated leather seats and all the bells and whistles. It even had wireless access to the internet. Her parents had paid almost a hundred grand for the custom SUV. And it wasn't the most expensive car in the cove. At least half the kids drove more expensive models. *I could only dream...*

If I was being honest, I would have been happy with a hooptie if I could have used it to escape some of the family get-togethers.

Crystal pulled into the car parking area, sliding in beside a red BMW convertible and a black Jeep, two of more than fifteen other cars there. There was also a variety of 4 wheel vehicles and three golf carts. The majority of the teens weren't old enough to drive, but inside the private cove, most did it anyway.

The Winters clan really believed in family gatherings. Not a week went by without some family event that required a mandatory appearance. The week after my accident was no different and a broken wrist did not excuse me from a cookout. I was beginning to wonder if I had died, would they have carried my embalmed body around like some crazy *Weekend at Bernie's* parody?

An offshoot of the drive led down a narrow track that curved around the back of the house before ending in a second large parking area just beyond the pool house. It was full too. And there were people everywhere.

Like every other house in the Cove, Nick and Elsa's house was huge. Like most of the homes in the Cove, it was a brick three-story, Federal styled Colonial, with a square-shaped central living area. Where our house had a single story, a mirrored pair of two-story wings swept out from each side. Tall columns and a wide curved staircase led up to an ornate set of double doors.

Elsa loved gardening and it showed. Thick vines of purple wisteria grew up one side of the entrance, winding its way around an upper balcony and over a pearl white lattice. Along the base of each wing grew colorful azaleas; red, pink, purple and white blooms a riot of color. The sickening sweet fragrance saturated the air, overpowering the fragrant odor of roasting meat, causing my already sensitive stomach to roil. Even with the car windows rolled up, the nauseating scent invaded my senses.

The guests were gathered near the pool house, either sitting in groups talking or playing in the sparkling water. A couple of the boys were about finished with setting up a net for volleyball and badminton games. And the latest songs were piped through a top o the line sound system. If I hadn't been so uncomfortable being around strangers, it would have been a great party.

I noticed two men in white uniforms manning an enormous stainless steel smoker. When one opened the smoker door, the tantalizing aroma of slow-cooked meat wafted throughout the air, drowning out the overly sweet scent of all the flowers. Intent on taking advantage of the heavenly aroma, I carefully scoped out a table location downwind from the smoker, hoping to make the most of the smoky breeze.

My injury would excuse me from the pool and most of the activities, but it was still going to be a long day.

Cody was doing his best to entertain me by

showing off on the diving board, trying various dives with different degrees of experience, some perfectly delivered, some with disastrous results. His latest attempt, a gainer with a twist, was one of his best dives but it was also one of the scariest. I waited until he rejoined me to comment.

"Whew! That was close. I thought you were going to hit your head on the board on that last dive."

"No, it just looks that way from here. Mom used to scream every time I tried one. Now she doesn't even look up."

He was so adorable, even soaking wet, with his hair slicked back away from his face. When his eyes met mine, my heart raced. Visions of the two of us entwined together, made me blush. As if he could read my mind, his eyes traveled from my eyes to my mouth. He grinned as I licked my lips nervously. We had been spending a lot of time together but Crystal or one of the other boys was always around. We had not been alone since the time at the lake. Not that we hadn't managed to snatch a kiss or two, we had, and it was great. Unfortunately, we had never talked about whether we were a couple or not. Nothing was official and until it was, we had to be careful no one saw us. The entire secret liaison scenario was getting old.

"Wanna go for a walk?" Cody reached out to take my hand and I felt a jolt run through my body. He must have felt it too because he was grinning sheepishly, as I slid from the chair to walk beside him. This was the first time he had showed affection in front of the family. *I wondered if he ever felt as nervous as I felt when I was around him?*

He held my hand as we walked toward the gardens and I couldn't help but smile. My heart dropped a little as I spotted Hannah and Robert sitting on a bench just inside the garden, but it didn't seem to bother Cody. I decided to ignore them and enjoy the time we had together.

Cody apparently had a destination in mind as we strolled along. He led me along a graveled path that followed the edge of a coy pond to a tiny alcove with a curved marble bench hidden between two willow trees. It was one of those places you would miss unless you knew it was there. Nestled in the shadowy darkness, we were in a world of our own.

I couldn't help but smile as he sat down and pulled me into his lap. Setting so close, I could feel his breath on my cheek. As he tilted my face toward him, my eyes closed, and my lips parted just enough for him to see the pink tip of my tongue. With a groan, his lips came down, softly at first, then harder as he pulled me into a deep passionate kiss. His hands were on my back and my fingers were entwined in his hair as he hungrily explored my mouth with his tongue, searching for every sensitive nook and cranny. His hands stroked along my back and sides, his kisses getting deeper and urgent.

My body was reacting in a way that I had never felt before. Instead of pulling away, I shifted my weight to get closer to him. I vaguely recalled hearing the haunting refrain from *Dancing with a Stranger* drifting on the breeze. Heavy breathing drowned out the party in the distance as I forgot my inhibitions and gave in to my inner demons. Just when I thought we might go too far, he pulled back, staring into my eyes as if he was looking for some answer hidden deep inside them.

Evidently, he found whatever he was looking for because he relaxed, and kissed me gently once again.

"I've been wanting to do that forever, but we always had a shadow."

"Well, I'm glad we finally shook our shadow."

He pulled my lips to his for another kiss that left me breathless and flushed, my mind full of thoughts best left for another time. Before it could become anything more than that, a loud clanging began.

"Dinner," he announced. "We have to go."

We walked back to the tables hand in hand. If anyone noticed our absence, they kept it to themselves, which was fine with me. I was too busy absorbing everything that had just happened.

I was amazed to discover I was looking forward to the barbeque. The food smelled so good. Even the overpowering scent of flowers that had previously overwhelmed my senses, seemed to have weakened into a light gentle aroma floating on the summer breeze. Crystal kept looking at us both and grinning. I wanted to ask her what she thought was so funny, but I was afraid I already knew the answer.

The waiter placed several plates of delicious smelling food on the table and my stomach rumbled its approval. For once, I was actually hungry and decided to concentrate on the food and not give anyone else a chance to comment.

The pitmaster had loaded up my plate with savory Memphis style rubbed ribs, thick slices of juicy beef brisket, and a mound of pulled pork, covered in a tasty honey-based sauce that enhanced the delicate smoky flavor. Great bowls of potato salad, coleslaw, and baked beans were shared amongst the diners family style. I was certain there was no way I could get another thing on my plate, then someone brought out trays of fresh corn soaked overnight in salt water, that had been smoked while still in its husk. Cody laughed and showed me how to twist the husk and pull it off in one piece. There was melted butter to drizzle on top. It was possibly the best corn I had ever eaten.

I didn't want to say or do anything to disturb the magic. Over the years, I had experienced too many times, how quickly things could go wrong. All it took was one cruel word or a single catty comment and a new relationship could fall apart.

The day had gone so well, I was disappointed when Crystal said she was ready to go. My eyes drifted to Hannah who was playing Uno with Robert and the twins and I understood. I had been in her position too many times.

Cody squeezed my hand. "I'll call you later when I get home. I need to tie up a few loose ends around here before I head that way." He didn't offer any details, but I had the strangest feeling it had something to do with Hannah and Robert. Either way, it wasn't my place to get involved.

Crystal didn't talk much on the ride home and I was glad. I wasn't sure I knew the answers to the questions I was certain she would ask and was pleased to avoid having to come up with a decent response. She left after promising to call me in the morning and I went straight to bed.

CHAPTER 14

THE TRUTH COMES OUT

"Hold on!" Crystal jerked up her emergency brake, sliding sideways in the road in an attempt to avoid hitting the huge oak tree head-on. The big SUV slowed enough for her to pull it out of the slide and allow it to roll to a gradual stop a few feet from the ancient oak. The only reason we had not slammed into the tree was the gentle rise in the road. If we had been going downhill when it happened, there would not have been a way to stop the truck before we hit the tree.

"Damn girl, what happened?"

"I don't know? My brakes stopped working and I could not slow down. "

"I knew we should have taken my car," Robert said.

Crystal glared at him but didn't reply. Her dad was meticulous about maintaining their vehicles. There was no way his mechanic would have missed a failing master cylinder. She dialed the garage and told Chip what had happened and asked him to bring a wrecker to retrieve the vehicle. We were only a few blocks from Roberts house, so it was no big deal to walk the rest of the way. Robert could give us a lift to Crystal's house and Cody could take me home later.

It had been a crazy day anyway. We had driven into Murphy to do some shopping. I had picked up a copy of a book I had been wanting to read and Crystal bought a new cellphone. Both the boys bought something, but neither would share what their purchases were. On the way home I convinced Crystal to swing through Cherokee, so I could grab some fudge. There was a tourist store there that sold some of the best I'd ever eaten.

I spotted a colorfully dressed native woman telling fortunes and I wanted to get mine told. My mother used to talk about going to see the beloved woman of the tribe and how she told her about my father years before she met him. Now I wanted to hear what she had to say about my upcoming birthday.

I took a seat on the blanket directly across from the soothsayer, studying the creases etched into her umber skin over the years. How many wonderful things had she experienced to earn such an interesting profile?

She seemed to understand my curiosity and take no offense. From a leather drawstring bag, she removed a handful of water-polished stones, each etched with a different symbol.

"Show me which one calls to you," she said. "The sand and the rune stones are simply tools that enable me to focus my gift in tangible ways. Some people use candles, others like crystal balls or tarot cards. My grandmother passed her knowledge on to me; as well as her rune stones. She got them from her grandmother. Today, I will read for you."

The runestones all looked similar in size and color. I had absolutely no idea what any of the unusual rune carvings meant; so I knew that pre-conceived ideas would not affect my decision. Instead, I closed my eyes and let instinct guide my choice.

She appeared surprised by the six stones I dropped into the sand before her. Whatever it was, it snapped her out of her prepared spiel into a different mindset. She stopped and studied me for a moment before speaking. "The patterns the stones make in the sand offers hints of the future. They can tell of life-altering events and repercussions of possible decisions to come. This reading is yours and only you should seek to understand what the stones reveal." She bent forward, studying the stones lying on the smooth white sand, a puzzled expression on her face. After a moment she began talking again.

"Look closely at the sand," she said. "You can see the pattern; telling of things past and of things to come. Most of the signs are in your favor. This one is a warning; a portent from the Gods to take care and protect yourself from harm. There are two symbols here, Isa, and Othila, both are dark reflections; preventing you from seeing the truth behind the shadows. One will be your downfall. The other is the start of a new life. You will need to look beyond the shadows to find who awaits to do you harm. The third stone is Thuri, it tells of changes to come. This stone is Ura or power, and in the combination with the glyph Pertha, it becomes stronger. Much power, more than anyone expects. This last one is the one puzzles me the most. The rune is Wunja. But it is inverted. Normally I would tell you that the danger would come from a stranger, yet this indicates someone close to you will be the source."

I thanked her for the reading and dropped a twenty dollar bill in the basket with the other contributions she had received. I wasn't too surprised by what she had said. Someone was always out to get me so the idea of it being a family member wasn't that farfetched. The fortune teller intrigued me. I could have easily spent the rest of the day watching and listening to everything she said.

I thought I had an idea what she meant by the two forces, but I really wasn't certain. Nor did her reading offer me any helpful advice regarding my birthday tomorrow. I was about to walk away when she stopped me. This time she didn't speak in riddles.

"You think you are alone, but you are not. The blood of the Aniyunwiya sings within you. Come back and visit the other side of your family. You will need our help to deal with the power you have been given. It burns within you and must soon be released. Everyone has a bit of the talent; it's just most don't bother learning how to harness the gift. Haven't you ever met someone you instantly knew was someone you needed to avoid? Or someone you felt comfortable around;

like you had known them all your life. That's a latent psychic ability. That power will test you in the days to come. Remember, we are here when you are ready."

She smiled, showing a mouth full of perfect teeth. "A gift." She reached into a pocket on her skirt and tossed me a leather bag, a smaller version of her own rune pouch.

" Something told me I would be needing this today."

"Thank you. What do they mean?" The bag held only four items. A red-veined dark green polished stone, a perfectly formed pink crystal, a feather and a chunk of dried root. I held the unusual items in my hand as she spoke, studying them so I could remember what she said about each one.

"I see a lot of pain hidden deep inside you. The crystal will draw that pain away, the Bloodstone will remove the source of the sadness from your life. The feather will lift your spirit, and the mandrake will protect you from further harm. Together they will strengthen you; I see a time of danger in the near future; keep the fetish bag nearby. I wear mine around my neck at all times."

Crystal kept looking at her watch and frowning, so I knew we needed to leave. I would have enjoyed spending more time talking with the old woman, but I had promised my aunt I would be home by dinner because there was a lot we had to do to prepare for my birthday. I thanked her again and tied the bag around my neck by the long leather strings. She seemed pleased by my response.

We all laughed about the strange reading once we were back in the Escalade heading for home. Today had been a good day so far and I didn't intend on letting the old woman's unusual reading ruin it. My birthday was tomorrow. I was going to have my very first birthday party. Cody was already making plans for next week, so I was reasonably sure he didn't intend to dump me in the near future. And he was the first guy I'd ever dated that I was hundo P about him liking me for me, instead of the possibility of an easy hookup. Crystal and Robert seemed to be doing okay. Basically, everything was good in my world. But I was still thinking about what she had said to me. The old woman's comments didn't bother me. I had learned to ignore snide remarks and catty innuendos made by petty vindictive people, a long time ago. True, she hadn't been inconsiderate or rude in any way, she had simply warned me of evil to come and the rise of some unusual power. I had no idea why she would say something so unusual to me, because I had listened to three other fortunes before she did mine, and they had nothing in common with my reading.

Robert was being a ham as usual about leaving Crystal. She puckered her lips and blew him a kiss. He reached up to catch it, held hit close to his heart, winked and tossed it back to her. *Saccharine sweet. Yuck.*

I waited until Crystal had said goodbye to Robert and we had piled into Cody's pickup and were on the way home before I mentioned how puzzled I was.

Crystal and Cody looked at each other. Then Cody spoke.

"It's not as crazy as it sounds. Has Peggy said anything to you about your birthday at all?"

"Not really. I mentioned getting my driver's license and she said to wait until all the excitement wore off, and then she would take me. She acted like it wasn't important and it kinda pissed me off. It is to me. I want to drive."

"And that's all she said about your birthday?" Crystal sounded surprised.

"She mentioned something about a birthday dinner but nothing specific. I didn't really expect anything. Not that I wasn't happy when you guys mentioned us celebrating that night."

Cody's eyes darkened. "This blackout has gone on long enough. I don't care what the Council says, it's only fair that you know what is coming. You only have two days left.

"Two days? My birthday? What's coming on my birthday?"

"Nothing bad, if we have anything to say about it," Crystal replied. "It's a long story but you need to know it. Cody is better at telling stories, so I will let him talk.

Cody grinned. "You might want to get comfortable. This is going to be a lot to take in all at once."

"Ok. Give me a sec to grab a coke." I made a quick pit stop to the bathroom and then flopped down on the sofa. There was something about the way they were acting that made me uncomfortable. I had no idea why it simply bothered me the way they kept glancing at each other. Finally, Cody started talking.

"It all started in Poland, before the second world war. A small group of genetic scientists was investigating the Rom, and their ability to tell the fortune of their customers. Don't get me wrong, most of the so-called seers were fakes, out to fleece the unwary for as much money as possible and move on to another town before anyone caught on. That group was called Gypsy's or Travelers. They weren't the group the scientists were interested in. Instead, they were concentrating on the rare few that seemed to actually be able to foretell the future in some small way. Official records said it was in an attempt to eliminate schizophrenia since that illness was nonexistent among the true Rom. However, there was nothing to substantiate that story and it was a fabricated rumor spread to cover up the real goal.

"The scientists discovered that the haplotype X2d6a in their DNA was the only commonality between them. This information was noted and shelved until Hitler decided to do intensive experiments, including breeding trials up and during World War II, in hopes of developing some type of metaphysical super soldier. Everyone thought the experiments a failure. And with all research records destroyed during the war at about the same time as Hitler's death, no one bothered to follow up. That wasn't exactly what happened."

He stopped talking to give me a chance to absorb what he had just said.

I was still slightly puzzled but nodded for him to go on. Maybe it would make more sense with more info.

Between 1936 and 1940 there were seventeen children born as a direct result of the experiments. No one is sure exactly what supplements or medications the parents were given during the pregnancy, but every child appeared physically flawless and mentally developed at above normal levels. They were all born with similar features, blonde hair, and an unusual shade of light blue eyes, perhaps slightly more attractive than the average, tall and well-muscled with no obvious visual flaws. Several of the attendant's wondered if there might have been some type of universal genetic material injected into each egg as it developed because of the similarities in appearance. Rumors of DNA from the shroud of Turin spread throughout the complex.

" You mean like the Jesus thingy?"

"Yeah, the cloth he was wrapped in."

"No way."

He grinned and started the story again. "When the bombs began dropping on Poland, the German army retreated. During the latter part of the war, chaos reigned over all that remained of Germany. The US and Allied armies were moving into position to take Berlin and it looked like the Allied forces were going to roll over Hitler and his army. The German hierarchy began to panic, and many took their own lives. Any sensible person quickly realized the Third Reich was rapidly coming to an end. The smart officers took off for South America and established new homes in Argentina and Brazil.

Dr. Zimv wanted to ensure the survival of his special children. He had been preparing for the need to escape the war zone long before the more obvious signs of impending destruction began to appear. With the help of four of his technicians, he slipped the children out of the county by boat only days before Szczecin's waterfront was razed. They traveled to Stockholm and that's where things became a bit jumbled.

He stopped and took a drink of his coke. " You got it so far?"

Well, other than the gobbled gook about DNA and a bunch of letters and numbers that I will never remember, I think so. This mad scientist did some kind of illegal experiment on a bunch of kids and they are my ancestors."

"Something like that. Anyway…Dr, Zimv's plan was to blend into the Swedish population, find temporary shelter, and then set sail for America at the earliest opportunity, where he hoped to embark on a new life.

Dr. Zimv, who was now going by the name Howard Winters, knew traveling with seventeen almost identical children would draw attention. Attention he didn't want. He decided to split the children up into family groups amongst his assistants. Their instructions were to make their way to Charleston S.C., in the United States, set up a household and wait to hear from him. There was already a large population of Dutch and Swiss ancestry in the area and he hoped having so many blondes in the area would enable him the time needed to establish himself and locate a safe home for his children. Each assistant was traveling with two girls and a boy. That left him with the odd group of three boys and a girl.

Dr. Winters was a pragmatic man who believed in being prepared for any eventuality. For years, out of every Reichsmark the Government allocated him to be spent on the experiment, half had been converted to US dollars and moved to an account in New York he'd earlier established in his name. He also managed to convert quite a bit of the money to easily carried gems. As the war continued, he began to buy gold, and have it deposited in the safety of the neutral Swiss banks. No one suspected he was using the Reich's own funds to set himself up comfortably in case of Germany's unanticipated failure.

Part of Dr. Winters plan came to fruition. He was able to travel with his family to New York, and from there to Charleston. He remained in the area until the war ended and then he located and purchased this valley. Of the seventeen children, fourteen were recovered as planned. They formed the seven original families here in the valley."

"So we are all related to each other?"

"Kinda," Crystal said. "But not that closely. That was in 1942. We are the fourth generation of children born to the seventeen original children."

"Yeah, Cody added, all of us are distant cousins but none are very closely related. The Council made sure of that over the years by sending some of the kids to Germany for college. Most of them hooked up with the locals.

Crystal had to get back into the conversation. "Plus, the children of the three that did not make it to America and their families were found after the war and they were brought to join the family here."

"So you are telling me we are kind of… like a creepy cult thing?

"No. Nothing like that. You can marry who-ever you want. There just one or two little details you need to know."

"Like?" I needed Crystal to be a little more specific. The story was hard to believe without the *'everybody is a cousin'* thing.

"If you leave the family, you leave the family money," she said.

"I kinda figured that. What else?"

"You can't leave until after you turn sixteen."

"Sixteen? Why not eighteen? That's the legal age of independence." Nothing about this story made sense. I was beginning to wonder if they were running some kind of con.

"That has nothing to do with it. And that's where Michael's story comes in."

"Okaaayyy?" It looked like I was finally go-ing to get some information about Michael. At this point I had more questions waiting to be an-swered than answers to questions already asked.

"No," Cody said. "This is not going to make

sense without you seeing for yourself. Crystal, get your car. We need to take a ride."

"Do you think she's ready?"

"We have three days. She has to be ready."

"So do you think…"

"I don't want to think that far ahead. It's possible." He watched as Memory crossed the room to join him. She had pulled her ebony hair back into a single tail hanging down her back to her hips. With her sun-kissed skin and native coloring, it was difficult to believe she was family, yet every test came back positive. She was his cousin, whether she resembled them or not. And that put her life in danger.

Crystal pulled up to the door and they climbed in. The cemetery wasn't far from the house, but she preferred to drive instead of walking.

Cody and I followed Crystal to the newest grave, Michaels, and watched as she laid a few fresh flowers on the snow white chipped marble that covered the soil. I took a minute to take in the headstone. Michal Bruce Winters, Born May 23, 2002. Died May 23, 2018. He had died on his sixteenth birthday.

I looked at Cody and he nodded. Then he led me to another grave a few away. Helen Diane

Winters, Born February 3, 2000. Died February 3, 2016. A heavy lump began to form in the pit of my stomach.

We wandered around the graveyard stopping in each families section to look at a grave. In each one there were several teenage deaths, each one on their birthday, each one at age sixteen. I also noticed something else and asked about it.

"This didn't start until the 1970s. What happened to set it off? Is there something in the water or is it a result of genetic inbreeding?"

"No. Neither reason. It has to do with the transition."

This was the third time I'd heard that word mentioned. Uncle Matt had shut Aunt Peggy down when she mentioned it right after I'd arrived. And Hannah had made a snide remark at the Lake about it. What was the transition? And how had it caused the death of so many of her relatives?

I kept my face as blank as possible as I prompted him to continue. "Transition?"

"I told you about the genetic experiments. Well...the object of the DNA manipulation wasn't just to produce Hitler's idea of perfect Aryan cousins. He was looking for much more.

The Rom were also heavily into metaphysics and magic. Magic intrigued Hitler. He wanted to know everything about it. He sent men all over the world to search out any verifiable artifact that could be tied to magic in any way. Most were worthless except for the entertainment value."

"Okay? What has that got to do with us?"

"Everything. One of the scientists studying DNA from an artifact found a link to the family haplotype and the Cherokee Indians. That is one of the reasons Dr. Winters moved to this area. He wanted to continue his study by adding the Cherokee's DNA to the children's bloodline. One of the last experiments he completed was on the second generation of children to be born in the United States during the late fifties and early sixties. They were the parents of the cousins you saw in the cemetery. All of them went through a transition when they turned sixteen. A lot of them died."

"Okay. Why sixteen? And what is the Transition?"

"Nobody knows why sixteen. We often wondered why not puberty? Women hit puberty earlier, so why don't they transition at fourteen? And why does it always happen on your birthday?

Same answer,--- no one knows. Some people display signs of impending change weeks or even months before the sixteenth birthday, but the change happens on the same day regardless of the portents."

"All right. Something is going to happen to me on my birthday. What?"

Crystal laughed. "That's the problem. No one knows. You are an enigma."

"I'm a whata?"

"A mystery," Cody said with a brief laugh. "No one knows what's going to happen to you. You are half Cherokee. Your DNA has much more of the haplotype than anyone in the family. You may hit sixteen and nothing happens. Or you may hit sixteen and the transition may kill you. Or---"

"Or?" So far, I hadn't heard anything to make me feel better about what was about to happen… or not happen… on my birthday.

---or, Crystal continued, "you may develop powers that none of the rest of us have."

"Powers?" What kind of powers? Phoenix on the X-men powers or I can tell you to kiss Cody and you will do it power?"

Cody looked right at me. " The kind that allowed you to hear what Crystal was thinking without her saying it out loud."

"Yep. Powers. That's me. I'm a telepath."

I looked around and Crystal was nowhere to be seen. Yet I had heard her as clearly as if she was standing next to me speaking into my ear.

"I'm over here by the angel statue. Look"

"I turned and she waved." *Damn.*

"Can you do it too?" I wanted answers, not more questions.

" No. I'm not a telepath. I'm a teleporter." He winked and disappeared, reappearing next to Crystal's car. He waved and then disappeared again, this time he reappeared next to Michaels grave. Crystal was standing beside him. They both looked pleased with themselves. At least they were walking back to me.

I waited for them to join me and then we walked away from the cemetery in silence. I had a lot to think about on the ride home.

Cody kept his arm around me, and I lay my head on his shoulder, thinking about what I had just seen and heard. It was a lot to take in at one time. I waited until we reached the house before saying anything, preferring to have solid ground under my feet before I asked any more questions.

But I really only had one.

"If these powers only come on after the transition on your birthday, then why can I hear Crystal talking now?"

"That's the one question we don't have an answer for. We haven't told any of the parents. It would scare the hell out of them. They have all adjusted to the scientific explanation of our powers, it's the metaphysical aspect that scares them. The change happening on the sixteenth birthday cannot be explained through science. That leaves Magic and there is no way any of them will accept that."

"Either way, I need to digest everything you told me." Magic had always intrigued me. My favorite books and movies all involved the paranormal in some form. Add a bit of mystery and you had me hooked forever. I even spent my hard earned money on a book of spells. I never really believed any of them would work, but the possibility was worth the expense. Besides… you never know what is real anyway. For all we know, we could all be figments of some bedridden paraplegic's dream."

Crystal broke out laughing. "You never know what the future holds. But keep your mind open.

Sometimes good things happen when you least expect them."

Yeah. And sometimes bad things happen…

CHAPTER 15

THE MINE TRAP

Whichever distant relative had designated the hidden valley as the perfect site to establish the Winters homesteads, had chosen its location well. The cove was the perfect place to grow up. My aunt and Uncles home was relatively high up on the slope of the mountain overlooking the collection of farms. From where I was standing, I had great views of the valley and the rocky hills that surrounded it on three sides as well as the main road that continued to the lake sparkling in the distance.

Things were finally coming together for me. After the trip to the cemetery, I now understood much more about my family and why they lived the way they did. And why they had wanted me to come home. The information scared me and excited me at the same time. Who wouldn't like the idea of having some kind of superpower? It was the possibility of death that made me nervous. Not that I had any say so in the matter.

It was evident that many of my new relations considered me a mongrel, little more than the half breed by-blow of a rebellious teenager and her indigenous lover. I was confident that once the newness had worn off their shiny new toy, they would ignore me completely.

I still had a lot of questions I wanted answered. But I could wait a few days before I brought them up. Once I reached my majority they had to answer me, even if they did not like the idea of telling the family secrets to a newcomer. The had set the rules and had to obey them.

At least Crystal was beginning to get over the sudden loss of her boyfriend. I had never known Michael, and it was really difficult to get anyone to speak about his death, but I had pieced together enough to know it had been sudden and unexpected.

Michael had died during the transition. And he wasn't the first to die. There were six graves in the family cemetery that were less than five years old. All had died on their sixteenth birthday. And I turn sixteen tomorrow. That scared the shit out of me. Was I going to die, too?

It wasn't as if I ever dwelled on the possibility

of dying. In direct opposition to my earlier plans, I had actually begun to look forward to the future. My birthday party was tomorrow afternoon and Cody was taking me out to dinner tonight. Now, if I could just find my pig, I could go inside and get ready for my date.

"Here piggy, piggy. Where are you? Princess, it's time to eat." I rattled the food in the bowl, expecting her to come running around the bushes at any moment. She never missed a meal.

I heard a squeal and then I saw princess charging around the bush like something was chasing her. Since there were coyotes in the nearby woods, I looked but didn't see any signs of an animal. The sound of boots scrunching on loose gravel drew my attention seconds before I caught sight of the two strangers. My initial impulse was to run but I hesitated. This wasn't the LA ghettos, this was a private cove in an exclusive neighborhood of the North Georgia Mountains. No one passed thru the front gates without permission. They looked kind of rough, but maybe they worked on the lawn team. I decided to ask them. If they had not passed thru the gates, it was possible they were hikers who had strayed off one of the public trails.

"Can I help you?" I noticed they were not carrying any tools.

"Is Mr. Winters at home?" one asked. The other held his hat in his hand, and I was struck by how polite they were. I immediately felt as if a weight had been lifted from my shoulders. They were here to see my Uncle Matt!

"Yes. Give me a second and I will get him for you." I made the mistake of turning my back to them to walk toward the door. My skin prickled with an almost animalistic premonition that something wasn't right; seconds before I felt my arms being clutched from behind by one, as the second slid his hand over my mouth. I struggled to escape, biting down on the finger of the hand over my mouth while I stomped as hard as I could on the arch of the man holding my arms. My overactive imagination was more than willing to provide me with a multitude of possible escapes as the man I'd bitten loosed my mouth.

"Bitch," he snapped, shaking his bloody finger.

Before I could do little more than gasp in a deep breath in preparation of a scream, I felt the sharp jab as a needle bit into my neck. Everything started spinning. Events from that time on became unclear. I vaguely remember going to my knees and then to the ground. A small part of my brain registered a closeup view of pea gravel and green grass before my vision greyed completely to black.

***

"She's awake." A man's voice.

"That doesn't change things. How long?" A woman?

"A few more minutes. If you have anything to say, now would be a good time to say it." A different man.

"No. Just hurry up. I want to be home before someone realizes she is gone." The woman, I could tell it was a female standing there even though I could not identify who was speaking, kept the pistol she held, pointed my way as she talked. I decided to take a chance and see if I could rattle her while I studied my surroundings. From my position on the ground, I could only see up to her chest. I could tell she was southern by her accent, but nothing else.

"You do realize I will be missed. No one is going to believe I disappeared right before my birthday." After my birthday maybe, but not the day before. My sweet sixteen was too important.

She stepped back toward the exit and I got my first view of her face. Well, the area where her face would be if she had not been wearing a black ski mask that hid everything except her mouth and eyes.

"I'm sure they will get over it." Her blue eyes flashed angrily before she managed to get her emotions back under control. Eyes I had seen too many times before. My mother's eyes, and the eyes of almost every female in the family.

"Sure, they will notice you are gone, but without a body, they will assume you took off. Maybe with one of the boys from the reservation like your mother. Not that it will make a difference to you. It may be too late to stop what's already happened but making sure you are dead tomorrow will definitely eliminate any interference from now on."

I could tell from her voice she was anxious to be done with her part of the scenario and gone. She hesitated, and that gave me a chance to see her finger tightening on the trigger. I threw my body to the left just as the gun went off.

***

My body lay in the shadows, as unmoving as a felled log. I had no idea how long I lay bleeding upon the ground before the men finally walked away. Neither had bothered checking to see if I was dead. The bullet had cut a glancing blow across my head slightly above my right ear. Between the dried blood and the muddy sludge from the wet blood mixing with the dirt on the floor of the cave, I was certain it looked bad enough for them to assume I was dead. It wasn't very bright in the tunnel and neither man seemed concerned with the unknown woman's ability to shoot straight. So I played dead, knowing that once I got out of this predicament, I could deal with the bitch. There was only so many women in the cove. I would recognize her when I was standing face to face and heard her speak, I was certain.

The two men had joked around, displaying none of the nervous behavior you would expect from men whose identity had been compromised when they followed her down the tunnel. They were confident that even if wasn't dead, I was seriously injured and would never live long enough to identify them.

Wrong, their faces were seared into my mind. I would have no trouble identifying them to the police once I reached safety. And I intended to escape. The million dollar question was how?

First, I have to get out of here…where ever 'here' was. My eyes had adjusted to the weak light, enough that I could see I was inside some type of tunnel. My mind instantly associated it with a mine of some type. The walls were hard-packed earth, slicked smooth by a trowel and braced every ten foot or so with a six by six uprights beneath a ceiling supported by 8 inch wide planks overhead. The sides were lined with additional bracing posts and stacks of rough-cut timber were scattered along the sides, as though whoever had been working had just stepped out for a moment and would be back at any time. The tunnel floor was dry and that was a lucky break because I could see the tracks in the dust approaching the area I was sitting in, and then leaving, going back in the direction that they had come. So I knew which direction led out. It wouldn't be easy to navigate it in the dark, but I could do it.

Then something sitting about ten feet away caught my eye, a small box with wires leading to it. I had seen enough movies to recognize a bomb when I saw one. That's what the men had been doing. The charge could be set for five minutes, fifteen minutes or an hour. It could go off in the heartbeat. There was no way to know and without a light, I was not about to attempt to look and see.

My heart tightened in my chest, and it suddenly became harder to breathe. Apparently 'she' wasn't going to leave the end of my life to chance. 'She' was going to bring the tunnel down on top of me. No wonder they were not worried about me being dead. They were planning on sealing me inside the tunnel either way.

Assuming my abductors had no intention of remaining in the mine and being buried with me, I figured I still had some time to get as far away from the epicenter of the explosion as possible. It may not be far enough, but the alternative was to lie there until the bomb went off and pray for a miracle. My life had not included a lot of those.

I squirmed to my knees and then to my feet, wove back and forth a little as I fought to get my balance, and then began running down the tunnel. As I ran along the tunnel, I could see a trail of indistinct footprints in the dust, some clear and easy to read, some with a second print superimposed atop an earlier one. Following the footprints brought me to a junction in the tunnel and my first problem. There was a clear trail entering and leaving both branches. I had no idea which way to turn. One thing I was certain of, I needed to get as far away from the site of the explosion as possible before it happened. That's when It clicked into my head. All I needed to do is follow the wire. Duh…

I felt around until I found it. My abductors had run it through the shadows along the base of the right wall. Once I had it in my hand I began running again, sliding the wire through my fingers as I followed it toward what I hoped would be a way out. I knew the blast could be triggered at any second. 'She' would not have gone to such an extreme if 'she' had no intention of following through with her threat. My only chance of survival was to put distance between me and the bomb and hope that the foundation of the tunnel around me survived. I had no idea how long it had been since the bomb was set. My gut told me I needed a lot more distance.

When the explosion came, I knew I was still too close to avoid the concussive blast. It slammed me into a wall. Hunched over from the pain in my shoulder, I ran as fast as I could, dogging falling rock and dirt until the pressure decreased. Somehow, I had avoided the main blast but that didn't mean I was out of danger. The rumbling sound grew louder, and a small amount of dirt fell from the ceiling overhead.

"Whoa!" I said out loud, grabbing wildly at the wall as the floor of the tunnel shook. I could hear cracks and pops as the overstrained supports gave out behind me. When it finally became apparent that the tunnel was going to come down, I threw my body forward, hoping to gain another three or four feet of distance. I pressed my body against a pile of bracing wood and prayed that the uprights would hold. Then a rock hit me in the head, and everything went dark.

***

I awoke to total darkness and air that was full of dust and hard to breathe. At first, I could not remember what had happened, and then slowly my mind filled in the blanks in my memory. *There had been a cave in. My own aunt had tried to kill me. I was alive.*

I attempted to move my arms and legs, checking to see if anything felt seriously injured. Other than a few twinges of pain from cramped muscles, everything appeared to be all right. The small shallow cavity surrounding me offered minimal room for movement, but at least I could shift around. And I could breathe. The air was moving, so the wind was getting into the area somewhere. There was no light at all.

I had no idea how long I had lain in the darkness before I regained consciousness. It was darker than I remembered so either it was night outside or any access to the outside was now blocked. I was not afraid of the dark but being trapped in a small area in the pitch black of a cave could shake anyone's resolve.

"Damn. Damn. Damn!" I screamed out loud, beating my hands against the ground in frustration

Loose dirt and rock fell from the ceiling above.

Get control of yourself and calm down! It is not helping your situation for you to just sit there and scream hysterically.

The passage behind me was completely blocked by fallen stone and dirt. The rocks and dirt had almost enclosed me, but my head was clear. I could tell there was room around my body, at least enough to maneuver. And I was facing in the right direction. Untying my shirt and wrapping it around my hands to protect them as much as possible; I started to dig fiercely, throwing the loose soil and rocks behind me, knowing that as each moment passed, the chances of my surviving decreased.

I used my legs to move forward through the narrow opening, pushing any small rocks away with my hands. Sweat blurred my vision and soon my hands had swollen so that they were unable to grasp the unwieldy rocks to pull them toward me. I stopped to rest and flex my fingers until I could use then again and then began digging once more. Diligently, I continued to creep forward inch by inch, until I no longer could feel the tunnel sides around me. I had no sense of time passing, it might have been minutes, hours or days.

I had reached a cavern; not a large one but one big enough to stand up and move easily between the walls. And best of all, there was a breeze, a small one but it was still fresh air, not the stale musty air I had been breathing for hours. The fresh air gave me hope. The possibility of escape had improved but I was exhausted.

I still intended to go on looking for a way out, but now I faced a more urgent problem. From my girl scout days, I knew I could go without food for days, but I needed water every day to survive. I was prepared to rest for an hour or two before continuing on, but finding water was now my first priority. Somehow, in the darkness, I had missed the point where the wire had turned off the main tunnel. There was no way to backtrack and find that exit. I would need to find another way out of the mine.

Then I spotted the lizard. It was fate. Against the darkness and the rocks, it was almost impossible to see until it moved.

The sight of the small brown lizard running along an indention in the stone was one of the brightest moments of my life. This was the kind of lizard that needed to be near water to survive. I immediately jumped up and started following it as it skittered across the rocks and sand, afraid that if I let it out of my sight for a moment it would fade away like a mirage from a story of the old west. The lizard seemed to be unconcerned with the bedraggled girl following it as it moved steadily along the base of the cave wall, heading toward a darker shadow near a small pile of rocks. Minutes later it disappeared from my view. I rushed forward across the broken surface of the cavern, unsure if it had merely climbed under the rocks for shelter or if it had passed them by and continued onward outside of my range of vision. In my rush I slipped on a patch of wet clay, turning my ankle in the process. The lizard was gone, but I was lying on the ground in what I could now see, was a damp creek bed. Elated at my good fortune I crawled along the path of the moisture. It curled along the base of the wall for about twenty feet, and then turned inward, ending at the base of a skinny crack in the solid rock of the cave.

I could feel a trickle of water under my hand as it dripped down into a natural bowl in the stone below. And better than that, I could see stars twinkling in the night sky way up above my head. The night sky was already lightening as dawn approached. It would be a hard climb up the crack, but I determined to do it.

The lizards were more than willing to show me the easiest way up. I struggled with myself once more; the impulsive part wanting to rush straight into the climb, the logical part pointing out the need for water and rest before attempting it. Thirst won out and I half slid, half climbed my way to the bottom of the rock pile and then made my way to the small pool of crystal clear water. I pushed my face to the water and slurped it up like a pony.

It must have been too cold. My thirst was satisfied, but I now struggled with a nagging headache, a sharp pulsing pain that came and went like the waves on the ocean.

It still needed rest and I needed to stay warm. There was not enough room to lie down comfortably in the small cavity. I sat with my back against the wall, wrapped my arms around my knees to conserve heat and lay my head atop my arms. I wasn't too uncomfortable, just a little cool and it was easily bearable.

The helpless rage I'd kept simmering in the back of my mind changed to resignation and then to a self-indulgent pity party. Tears welled up in my eyes and I angrily wiped them away. The women in my family were strong and I would not allow myself to cry. I had never seen my mother cry, not even when she realized my father had died in the accident. She acted like she was alright as the paramedics worked to release her battered body from the wreckage because she didn't want me to be afraid. I would not disrespect her memory by allowing the tears to flow.

Somehow, I had done something to make this unknown woman hate me enough to want me dead. Why she had set up such an elaborate method to bring about my death, continued to elude me. The men could have shot me in the yard. She could have shot me in the yard. I could think of a dozen ways to kill me without going to such extreme measures. Obviously, she wanted to hide my death as long as possible.

I could see the stars fading in the sky over my head. Once the sun came up, I would begin climbing out. I was under no misconception that it would be easy. I was not an especially athletic type. Cheerleading had been about the extent of my sports participation. But I figured, if I did not get out of the hole I would die. At the least, my attempting the climb offered me a possible escape. And once I got out, I was going to find out who 'she' was. And the bitch was going to be sorry she ever thought about trying to kill me.

The last thought I had before I finally drifted off to sleep was that it was one hell of a way to start my birthday

***

My restless dreams spun fantasies of a perfect birthday---scenes of dancing at my party with Cody, followed up by chili dogs at the Varsity, and the simple pleasure of sharing a banana split with extra whipped cream to end the evening.

The harsh reality upon waking quickly grounded my mind to the facts of the true situation, especially the lack of a corner drugstore to purchase a bottle of pain killers to relieve the headache that had grown progressively worse over time. The sharp pains were almost constant now, wave after wave of pain that caused me to clench my teeth and pull up my arms toward my chest as each hit. And my imagination was starting to play tricks, as the pain increased, I started to hear voices, at first loud in my mind, then steadily growing weaker as time went by.

Kneeling beside the small shaft, I thought about my old scoutmasters' rules, especially the one about how you should never enter a cave without a partner. Nor go climbing alone. Somehow, I did not think the lizard would qualify.

I could see the bright blue sky clearly, but it was a long way to the top and I did not have any tools to help me climb. There was a small ledge about halfway up, so I picked that as a midpoint goal. Once I reached it, I would stop and rest before continuing my climb.

Taking a deep breath to steady my nerves, I gripped the first uneven section tightly and began to climb. At first, it was easy, the uneven surface made it possible for me to place my hands and feet securely. But then the passage walls got closer together, making it necessary for me to push my back against one side and use my legs to cross brace as I wormed my way up. Thankfully, I reached the ledge and pulled myself up, intending to sit back and take a nap. Except the ledge did not have a back to sit against; instead, there was a small dark opening. I vaguely remembered reading somewhere that miners often cut airshafts to the outside. This tunnel was much smaller than the main shaft that had collapsed but I could feel a steady breeze against my face and the angle of the slope was upward. I began crawling hoping it would not get smaller near the top. Less than fifteen minutes passed before I was sticking my head out of the airshaft to see where I was.

The feel of the warm sun on my skin was almost intoxicating after being in the stale underground air for so long. But that feeling paled beside the sight of a busy highway less than a mile to the south. If I wasn't so tired it would be great. I really missed my bed. The last thing I thought about before falling asleep was how wonderful it would be to see the smirk wiped off Hannah's face when I walked thru the door.

CHAPTER 16

SWEET SIXTEEN?

No!

My eyes flew open, my heart racing, as I struggled to catch my breath. It all must have been a dream. But it had seemed so real. I squeezed my eyes tightly and held my breath, then breathed out and in again deeply, holding it for the count of ten before I repeated the deep breathing exercise. My heartbeat had slowed, and I no longer felt like the world was spinning away from me. I wondered what had brought on such a terrifying nightmare. Was it the trip to the cemetery or was that part of the dream too?

The clock by my bed said ten thirty. That was strange, I was usually up and in the shower by eight every morning. Aunt Peggy must have decided to let me sleep in for my birthday. Smiling I snuggled back down into my covers, enjoying the sensation of the expensive linens against my skin. My skin? Where were my pajamas? I threw back the comforter and reached for my robe, then dropped my arm, staring at the mud-covered jeans and bra I was wearing. I was even wearing my boots! The crisp white sheets were streaked with a mixture of red clay, blood, and dust from what remained of my clothes.

Horrified, I swung my filthy boots away from the bed, doing my best to avoid getting anything else on the pastel bedding. Was it all real? And if it was real, how did I get from the mine to my bed?

I needed some answers. I searched for my cell phone before I remembered it had been taken by the two men. There was a landline, but I didn't have Crystal's phone number. I didn't have any-one's number.

Think girl, get your head together. You can't let your emotions control you. Cody and Crystal will know what to do about your troubles. First, take a shower and change clothes. Then you can head to their house and tell them everything that has happened.

I headed for the bathroom for a quick shower, eager to get to the bottom of all the mysteries. Ten minutes later I was clean, dressed and ready to go. The house was strangely quiet.

I passed my aunt and uncles room on the way to the staircase, but no one was inside the room. Hannah's bed was unmade, and she was not inside her room either. Could they have been taken too? Were the men still round the house?

I crept silently down the staircase, leaned around the corner and checked out the main rooms. Empty. Evidently, everyone had left before I returned. Even if my aunt and uncle were not home, I expected to find Dodi in the kitchen, but it was empty and there were no signs that she had been in at all. Weird.

I noticed the keys to the ATV were hanging on the hook as usual. That would take care of one vital problem, how I was going to get to Cody and Crystal's house. So far, this had been the craziest birthday I could remember. I still had no idea how I had gotten home, but the muddy clothes were undeniable proof that something had happened. It wasn't a bad dream, someone had tried to kill me. I was pretty sure it was one of my female relatives. I was determined to figure out which one had pulled the trigger. Next time she might be a better shot.

I entered the garage from the kitchen, flipping

on the overhead light so I could see to open the garage door to get the heavy four-wheeler out. I was surprised to see Princess inside her pen instead of loose in the yard. Someone had thought to bring her inside and give her food and water. Wanting to spoil her a bit because I hadn't been around to take care of her myself, I ducked back into the kitchen and snagged her a bunch of grapes. She showed her appreciation by peeing on my shoe. That's one thing about pigs I hated, a female pig will pee to show how much they love you. According to the vet, it's a great honor. The vet wears ancient boots, not a hundred and eighty dollar Nikes.

After being attacked by hornets, slung off a maddened horse and having a mine caved in atop me, this odd sign of affection was not enough to slow me down. I scratched behind her ears and hopped on the ATV. The garage had an automatic shut mechanism, so I wasn't worried about closing it behind me. It was around eleven o'clock. Normally, Crystal would have already made an appearance to roust me out of bed. I had no idea why she'd picked my birthday to ignore me, but I was certain she would have a good excuse when I arrived at her home. The path across the meadow would cut off half the distance. I figured ten minutes to cross the fields and then a half a mile down the main road to their house. Twenty minutes, a half hour at the most.

I was looking forward to seeing Cody. He was probably pissed at me for ignoring his calls. He had no way of knowing they had taken my phone.

I slowed to a stop at the top of the hill above their house. Something must have happened. Their yard was full of vehicles and most of my teenaged cousins were gathered on the steps outside. My hands began shaking. The only time I had ever seen that many people gathered together was for a funeral. Who had died?

I was suddenly overcome by fear, unable to believe something might have happened to one of the two people in the Cove I had come to care about. For just a second, I found myself hoping it was one of their parents and not one of them. Then I was riddled by guilt as the reality of what I had been thinking kicked in. How could I even think it would be better if one of their parents had died. No one deserved to go through the pain of losing a parent like I had experienced, especially Crystal or Cody.

The ATV started cutting out as I started down

the final stretch to the driveway. That's when I realized I had forgotten to check the gas in the tank before taking off. The motor finally gave up the ghost less than a block from the house, so I took the keys and walked, cutting across the backfield to reach the house. As I wove my way through all the parked vehicles, I realized everyone in the Valley must be here. I noticed Uncle Matt's black pickup and Hannah's red convertible as well as the silver Lexus Uncle Hugo usually drove parked near the front of the building.

I was no longer concerned it was a funeral. I could see Coral in shorts and Dane or Danny, was wearing jogging pants and a t-shirt; definitely not mourning wear. And by the shocked expression on Corals face, she had just seen me.

***

"You have no idea how much trouble you are in." My Uncle Hugo was livid. Unfortunately, I was the object of his angry tirade. "Your impulsive decision to take off has caused everyone in the valley distress. Not to mention how upset your aunt and uncle have been. Crystal and Cody will be grounded for months because of their bad decisions. Now we have to decide what to do about you."

Take off? I hesitated before speaking, a little stunned by the vehemence in his words. My head was killing me, the voices in my mind continued to bombard me with irreverent bits of conversation from people not in the room and it did nothing to ease the headache I had been dealing with all night. How much of the pain was from the bullet and how much from the birthday gift I'd received from my parents, I didn't know. I hadn't thought to ask many questions about the transition process itself.

"What to do about me? You need to catch the men who kidnapped me! And the crazy woman who shot me. I'm not the one who needs punishment. What kind of insane thought process came up with that brilliant idea?"

I was happy to see the angry expression fad from his face. It was immediately replaced by puzzlement.

"Kidnapped? We were told you had run away. That you were going back to the west coast and wanted no further contact by the family."

"Why would I do that? And what fool said I was leaving?"

"You did."

"No way! Somebody has a warped sense of

humor." I winced as another flash of pain racked my head. I closed my eyes, but it did not help.

I sat on the sofa and let him rant, doing my best to wrap my head around what he was saying. For some reason that I had not yet divined from his spiel, he was under the assumption that I had taken off for California. Cody and Crystal had been blamed for my vanishing act since they had gone against family wishes and divulged information about the family that was not supposed to be discussed under any circumstance.

They were in their rooms, grounded and I was not going to be able to talk to them until the family decided what to do with me.

" Do you have anything for pain. My head is killing me. I guess the bullet might have done more damage than I thought."

"Bullet? What bullet?"

I had his complete attention now. I pulled the hair away from my head, allowing him to see the raw crease in my skin. He examined my head for a moment and his entire demeanor changed.

"Sit here. Do not move. Keep your head as still as possible. That bullet needs to come out."

Bullet? Out? I thought it was out.

He pulled out his cell phone and made a call. I

heard him say he needed an officer immediately. He said yes and kidnapped to whoever he was speaking too before he hung up. Then he walked outside.

***

The next hour was crazy.

Hugo had sent most of the family home. Uncle Matt and Nick were still there, as well as Antonia, Hugo's wife, and Ulrika, Nicks sister.

According to Hugo, they were the Council Elders and they would be making the final decisions about my fate. While they argued between themselves about what to do about me, I decided to try and contact Cody.

Cody? Can you hear me?

Mem? Where are you? Everyone has freaked over you leaving. I've been calling you for hours.

They took my phone. Sorry.

Who took your phone?

I don't know their names. You won't believe what I've been through. I was kidnapped. And this woman tried to shoot me. Then they literally blew up a mine with me inside it.

Kidnapped? Then why did you send me and Crystal a text that you were going back to Cali-

fornia?

Wasn't me. They took my phone, remember?

Duh...Wait a minute, I'm coming down there.

I sat quietly until he came bounding down the stairs, then I threw myself into his arms and tears began to fall. He stood there and held me, while I cried out all the misery I had suffered, during the last fifteen hours. I could hear the adults asking Cody how he knew I was downstairs and him telling them I had contacted him. Crystal had also overheard our conversation and she was now standing behind me, with her arms around my shoulders.

"Let me make sure I'm understanding what you are saying. Memory spoke to you?"

"Yes. Today is her sixteenth birthday remember?"

Memory? Can you hear me? If you can, raise your right hand.

It was my uncle Matt. Since I was looking right at him, I could tell his lips had not moved. Either he was a very talented ventriloquist, or he was telepathic. Shrugging, I raised my right hand. *Would you like me to hop on one foot too?*

Matt paled.

The women began whispering amongst themselves.

Aunt Peggy grabbed Uncle Matts hand, and both looked like they were about to be sick.

I didn't understand it. They were acting like something catastrophic was about to happen. In my opinion, it already had. I was the one who had a mine dropped on their head.

"Memory come sit down and tell us all happened to you. There's obviously been a miscommunication of some sort. We need to know the entire story." Hugo's voice quavered. His eyes were locked on Matt and Peggy as he spoke.

They were still pale as ghosts but at least they were no longer clinging to each other.

I quickly described my experiences of the last fifteen hours, starting with the men in the yard and the needle, to the woman in the mine shaft, the bomb and finally to waking up in my bed to an empty house.

The longer I talked the angrier Hugo became. Ulrika and Antonia were staring at me as if they were expecting something crazy to happen at any moment.

I noticed Nick was watching my aunt Peggy, but my uncle Matt was being ignored.

That surprised me until I realized it had also clicked into their minds that one of the women in the family had tried to kill me.

Hugo had Antonia look at the raw flesh where the bullet had grazed my head. Antonia was a doctor, a general practitioner, but she only treated the family. She left the room long enough to fetch her medical bag. She used a swab to apply a numbing agent, then deadened the area near the bullet with lidocaine. I didn't even feel the slight nick of the knife. The bullet popped right out. It had not penetrated the bone, just skin, and some muscle. After two stitches to close, she was done. She mentioned an x-ray and Hugo told her to schedule it with the doctor for later that afternoon. Then he turned back to me.

Hugo smiled. "I need you to trust me. Will you? I want to try an experiment."

"Sure?" I was puzzled by his statement. Was he going to hypnotize me or something?

He walked over and laid his hand on my shoulder. A second later we were standing in my living room. In my house. Over a mile away.

He smiled. "I'm a jumper. I can move from one place to another. I want to take a look at your room. "

It was a strange request, but I figured what the hell and showed him the way. Once we were inside the room he walked straight to my bed and flipped back the comforter, studying in the mud and blood stained sheets. Once he was satisfied that part of my story was true, he asked to see my clothes and boots. I had left them in the bathroom, and they were still sitting beside the tub. Hugo picked up the boots and rolled the jeans around them. Then he laid his hand back on my shoulder and we returned to Nicks house. We couldn't have been gone over five minutes, but it was clear to me the others had been discussing the turn of events while we were gone.

Crystal and Cody were now sitting on the loveseat and the adults were gathered around the poker table talking. Hugo walked to the table and dropped his bundle without saying a word. Ulrika unrolled the jeans, her mouth tightening at the blood stains. Then she laid her hands on the jeans and closed her eyes.

She stayed that way for about five minutes then shook her head. " I can tell it's a mine, and I can get a general area but nothing exact. Its somewhere in the National Forest, but not in an area that touches our land."

"We need more than that to find it." Matt looked at Peggy and she shook her head.

"Do you want to try and read Memory?"

"I don't know if I can. I don't know if I even want to try." She looked scared, and that made me nervous. Why would she be scared of me? I had no reason not to show them the mine. It wasn't that hard to find.

"I can show you where the mine is if you want to see it. I'm not sure if you will fit down the air-shaft but you could probably port inside."

They all turned to look at me.

"How do you know where it's at? You said you were unconscious when the moved you."

"I don't know where the entrance is. But I do know where the airshaft came out. I could see a store from the ridge side. It was called Maguires Bait and Beer."

"That's on old 64. About halfway to Copper-hill. We can be there in half an hour." Hugo began issuing orders to everyone.

"We'll take my truck. Cody, you can ride with us. There's room for five. Antonia can stay her with Eka and Peggy. You don't mind, do you baby?"

"No, of course not. Just get to the bottom of

this. We can take care of the rest later. It's obvious she's already transitioned. The question is into what?"

That statement caught my attention...*into what*? I wasn't sure I like hearing that. This had been the strangest sweet sixteen I could imagine. And if the last hour was a sample of what the rest of the day would be like, I wasn't sure I was ready for it.

***

Less than a half hour later we pulled into the parking lot. It was the store I had seen from my perch before falling asleep. I had a really good idea where I had come out and was able to direct Hugo to the access port. Just as I suspected, there was no way he was going to be able to fit down the air vent.

It turned out it wouldn't be necessary. Hugo looked around the Ridgeline and located the crack I had climbed up. He was able to teleport down into the small chamber below. There he found the remains of my bloody t-shirt. He was back in a matter of minutes.

The look on his face said everything. He went into a huddle with Matt and Nick for a few minutes and then he looked at a map the owner of the store had drawn for Nick while we were gone. Mr. Maguire seemed to be certain the entrance to the old mine was located along the back side of the ridge on a section of private property right before the entrance to the National forest. He said at one time it had been a profitable gold mining operation until the vein played out. It had been closed for over thirty years. As far as he knew, the same family had owned the land for generations; but he had no idea who they were.

The men's conversation ended, and they began walking toward the pickup. Nick waved for us to join them.

"We are going to drive over to the old mine entrance and see what we can discover. There may be something there that would explain why you were targeted…and by who."

We had no problem locating the mine. There was a faded wooden sign on the fence saying Pierson Mining Co., No Trespassing. Unfortunately, there was a heavy lock on the chain link fence that prohibited us from driving onto the property.

Hugo ported inside the gate and walked up the old road until he could check out the mine shack before vanishing again. He was back about five minutes later. His lips were set tight and his brow was furrowed as if he was mentally debating discussing what he had seen. He must have decided against it because he kept whatever information he'd found to himself.

Once we were on the road heading back to the cove, I could tell Nick was discussing something with him because there was a light buzz in the back of my mind. Evidently, there was a way to block me from hearing the conversation. I added that to the list of questions I wanted to ask about my new power. For now, I was happy to have Cody's arm around me. I was still feeling the effects of the last 24 hours and it took all my concentration not to fall asleep.

It didn't work.

***

Cody gently shook me awake, careful not to startle me by moving too quickly. We were sitting in the drive in front of his house once again. I could see the grownups sitting on the front steps. They were talking about everything that had been learned during our trip to the mine.

Antonia appeared angry. She was waving her hands, emphasizing whatever she had said with sharp movements. It was easy to tell she was upset about something, even if I could not hear her words. Not that I cared. I was alive and intended to stay that way. Sticking my nose into another person's business had not worked out so well in the past.

Cody took advantage of the lack of grownup attention to pull me into his arms for my first birthday kiss. It didn't last long enough to satisfy me, but it did take the raw edge off my disappointment over how the day had gone so far.

"How are you feeling," he asked. "I know this has got to be hard to deal with. I can't imagine someone trying to kill me, especially while I was going through the transition."

"Yeah. Do me a favor. Everyone keeps saying transition. What to hell do they mean?"

Cody smiled. " I forgot to tell you that part, didn't I. We were going to talk about it last night, but when you didn't call, I jumped to the conclusion you didn't want to talk to me. I'm sorry, you were scared and alone; while I was pouting."

"It's no big deal. I'm more concerned about what's about to happen. What is transition?"

"That's the problem. We don't know what's going to happen. You should have been a mover. That's what your mother was. She could cause atoms to speed up or slow down."

"That's a power?"

"Sure, think about it. Everything is made of atoms. The only difference in a solid and a liquid is how fast they are moving and how far apart they are. Your mom could walk through solid walls. She had a strong telekinetic gift, she could start a fire by speeding up atoms or cause it to rain by slowing them down. Everyone was prepared for that. Not telepathy. Or teleportation. No one ever gets more than one power. So far, you have teleportation and telepathy.

He stopped talking and appeared to be thinking about what he was going to next. "Normally when someone goes through the transition the parents are there to help keep it under control. Your aunt Peggy is as close as they could get. She gets glimpses of what someone is thinking but has no real control. The council asked her to prepare you for today."

"As if. She never even mentioned what was going to happen."

"That's the reason for the meeting today. When you vanished, everyone was scared the secret would get out."

"So what went wrong with me?" I reached for

my coke and took a drink. I was so thirsty. I wondered if that was one of the side effects of transition. I was hungry too, I hadn't had breakfast and now it was past time for lunch.

"Uhhhh, I don't think anything went wrong."

"Oh well, I guess I will have to wait and see what happens. So far, the only thing that has bothered me is my appetite. Do you have anything to eat inside? I'm starving?"

"I'm sure I can find you something. Wait here, I'll be right back."

He was back in a few minutes with a thick roast beef sandwich and some potato chips. I took a big bite and sighed, it tasted soooo good. There was something about pigging out while lying against your boyfriend that simply felt right. I wished I had thought to ask for another coke, mine was almost gone.

Cody must have been reading my mind because he passed me a cold can without me asking. I popped the top and drank half before stopping. A few chips later and I was ready to continue our conversation.

"So give. And details please."

"I'm about 90% certain you are a mover like your mother," he said. So that's three powers.

Possibly four, since you mentioned having a feeling that something isn't right. That could be precognition."

"Okay rewind. Why do you think I'm a mover?"

"Because you finished your coke and I tossed the can out as we passed the main gate."

"Then how did I---" I stopped talking, Cody was grinning from ear to ear and I had a good idea why. But I asked anyway to make sure.

"You didn't bring me a new coke, did you?"

He shook his head.

Oh, shit. "What should I do? Should we tell them?"

"I don't know. Normally when someone is going through the transition, they are separated from everyone so that no one could get hurt if they can't control their powers. But you don't seem to be having any difficulty at all. And you have more than one power. I've never heard of that before. Maybe it was because of your father's blood?"

"Who knows? I certainly don't. All I was hoping to get for my birthday was a car."

I watched as Hugo and Nick approached the truck. Both men looked upset. Things didn't look so good from where I was sitting. Maybe I was about to get grounded. That would be about par for my birthday.

Hugo cranked the truck without saying anything. Nick shook his head at Cody's unspoken question and simply reached for his seatbelt. Cody sighed and did the same thing. That required me to change positions since there was no way I could be strapped in while lying in his lap. We were already moving before I managed to click the belt into place and neither man had said a word. I had no idea where we were going, or what was going to happen, once we arrived. I was scared I wouldn't like the answers.

CHAPTER 17

TALK WITH HUGO

They postponed my birthday celebration.

It hurt my feelings, but I did my best to try and understand their point of view. They had been prepared to deal with a mover, the nickname for a someone with the telekinetic ability to move objects through mental manipulation. So you can imagine their surprise when I manifested the ability to speak teleport.

So far, we have been able to hide the other surprises. Crystal and Cody made it clear to me that the longer I can keep my powers a secret, the better my control will be when I have to display them to the council.

Not that everything has gone smoothly. Far from it. I spent the next few days in isolation. Finally, three days after my birthday Hugo had called, asking me to come to his home. I was a nervous wreck. It had been four days since the attempt on my life. He wanted to discuss this and a few other minor issues, as he put it.

It seems, under family law, I was no longer under the strict guidance of my Aunt Peggy and Uncle Matias. Uncle Matt had offered to go with me for emotional support, but I told him I could handle it. Now I wondered if that might not have been the smartest move. He had offered me the use of the extra car and that was nice. As long as I stayed inside the valley, it allowed me to practice driving without being under the jurisdiction of the police. I wanted my license, so I took every offered opportunity to drive.

My stomach was doing flip flops by the time I pulled into the driveway at Hugo and Antonia's house. Unlike most of the homes in the valley, their house was a modern ranch style without all the elaborate flourishes common to the much larger mansions. I liked it better than the fancy Georgian mansions most of the family lived in.

I tilted the mirror down and checked my appearance, feeling as if I was going to some type of interview instead of a simple visit with a family member. Noticing how much I was sweating, I wiped my palms on my jeans and knocked at the door.

Antonia opened it and invited me inside. I instantly fell in love with their home. It was every-thing I always wanted, and more. Instead of the cold formality of my aunt and uncles place, their home was built around a central great room with an enormous fireplace. The entire back wall of the great room was glass. You could stare out that wall for days and never grow tired of the view. They had decorated it with comfort in mind in-stead of style. Two comfortable couches flanked the fireplace, both enhanced by colorful throw pillows. A second seating area held three over-sized recliners and a gigantic flat screen televi-sion. Hugo was sprawled out in one, a portable table draped across his lap, and a cup of some-thing hot steaming in his hand. He returned his cup to the tray and set it aside as I entered.

Antonia offered me something to drink and then indicated I should make myself comfortable in one of the recliners. She returned with my iced tea and then seated herself in the remaining chair, sipping on her drink.

I sipped and smiled, many people ruined the taste of tea by smothering it with too much sugar. Hers had just the perfect amount, sweet enough to dull the bitter undertaste, but not so sweet you could stand a spoon upright inside and it wouldn't fall over.

"How have you been?" Uncle Hugo offered me the briefest of grins, the perfect amount to seem interested without seeming fake. I knew he meant since my abduction, so I answered his unspoken question.

"I still have trouble sleeping through the night but most of the physical damage has faded. "

"That's good. I have discussed your situation with several members of the family and have decided you deserve to understand the possible reasons behind the attack. We have a good idea who the woman is, but we are undecided on what steps to take."

That got my attention. I sat up a bit and leaned slightly forward and he continued.

"The important thing is your safety."

"Why did she do it? It's not like I ever did anything to hurt her."

His eyes softened. "You hurt her when you were born. You had no control of it. I know that Cody and Crystal have explained the basic information but there is a lot they do not know. They understand that they now receive a portion of the family assets. What they do know is that all assets are divided among surviving family members according to their ancestral line. My wife and I were blessed with the kids late in our life, and they will inherit my portion of my line as well as from Antonia's side of the family. You know that your mother was the eldest and she inherited from both her mother and her father. Peggy inherited from her mother, however, her father never developed his powers and chose to leave the compound before her mother realized she was pregnant with your aunt Peggy. His share of the family money went back into the general pool and was divided among the rest of the family. Now that you are of age, you will be able to access your share of the assets ." He smiled again. " You are extremely wealthy."

"How wealthy is extremely wealthy?"

He laughed. "Would you believe you are the wealthiest person in the valley?"

"No shit?" I slapped my hand over my mouth, blushing hotly and he broke out laughing.

I waited until he stopped. "Having money is nice, but it does not explain why someone would try to kill me."

"It comes down to timing. If you had died before your powers were manifest, your money would have been split among the remaining families. Sad as it is for me to admit, many of your relatives were not happy when you were discovered. It put quite a monkey wrench in quite a few of your cousins' plans for their share of the money."

"So she tried to kill me because she wanted money I didn't even know about? To keep me from getting it?"

"That's the best guess scenario. There are a few branches of the family that did not manage their funds as well as the others."

"So what should I do? Forget about it and act like it never happened?" *Over my dead body. I was going to find the bitch and make her pay. The money wasn't the point. She shot me and tried to blow me up!*

" It would be good if you could, but I understand that might be difficult to do at this time."

I simply nodded. *Hell no. I wanted names.*

"Changing the subject, we need to discuss your powers." He raised one eyebrow and Antonia nodded.

My heart fell. He had said powers, not power. How much did he know? I decided to stay quiet and let him talk. Maybe it was a slip of the tongue. We had been very careful about where

I practiced; going outside the valley to an abandoned rock quarry about ten miles down the road that Cody's uncle owned.

Suddenly my empty tea glass toppled over and fell toward the floor. Without thinking, I froze it, right before it would have hit the ground. Realizing I had made a mistake I withdrew my mental grab to allow it to fall the last inch or so. Instead, the glass floated upward and landed in Antonia's outstretched hand.

Uncle Hugo nodded.

"So you are definitely telepathic and telekinetic. I also expect you can teleport since you were able to jump with me. That's only possible when both can port. If you didn't have the ability, you have remained in the same location while I ported away."

"So you knew I had more than one power on my birthday?"

"Yes. But we wanted to see how you did on your own. I have to admit, you kids were clever, going out to Peter's quarry was a brilliant idea. You should have checked for security cameras, but it was still a good idea. No one close by to get hurt while you experiment. "

"Just how much did you see?"

"Enough to know not to piss you off. I'm not sure which scared me the most, the fire tornado or the snowstorm in August."

"We were careful. Cody made sure they were far enough away not to get hurt if anything went wrong." That wasn't entirely true. The first time I used TK to make fire, I set fire to one of the trees and I had to pull half the water in the quarry out to make sure it didn't spread. And I was certain he hadn't been in the truck with us while we making out last night. We had steamed up the windows to the point that we were both soaking wet by the time common sense took over and we decided to call it a night. Cody had to roll down the windows and use his shirt to dry off the windshield to drive home.

"How about Clairvoyance? Have you had any unusual dreams? Or heard any strange voices?"

"That depends, I have been hearing voices for weeks now, but I thought it was my imagination. Could I have been hearing real people talking?" Now I was worried. Some of the things I overheard were not exactly warm thoughts and loving comments. If someone really felt that way about me, I needed to keep a sharp eye out.

"For now, let's assume you were picking up

stray thoughts from people around you. Learning to handle three powers will be hard enough for you to handle. We don't want to pile any more on you than is necessary. "

"Thanks, I guess. I have a question. You jump blind. Don't you ever worry about landing in a tree or a wall?" Whew. He didn't know about my premonitions. Or my ability to find anyone or anything I had touched. And I was pretty sure I could walk outside my body. And once I got to the cave entrance, I looked back toward the store and realized I could not read the name. There was a good possibility I could add farseeing to the list. The longer I could keep the other skills secret the better it would be.

"It doesn't work like that. If I tried to jump to a place where space was already occupied, I would simply return to the original location. You can't reassemble inside a rock or a tree. Or at least I have never heard of anyone doing that."

I watched his face and he appeared to be thinking deeply about the possibility. One of the things I intended to practice in the future was passing through a solid wall. I decided not to mention that to Uncle Hugo at this time. He already had enough on his plate without me adding anything to it. I was getting pretty good at speeding up and slowing down atoms. Moving them father apart shouldn't be that difficult. Of course, I still needed clarification of one tiny detail.

"Can I get me a car?"

Antonia broke out laughing and gave me a hug. Hugo was doing his best to hold his in, but finally, he gave up and began laughing too.

"What's so funny?"

"I bet your aunt Antonia that would be the first question you asked other than about the kidnapping. You just cost me a trip to Atlanta. She's had her eye on a ring she saw at a store in Buckhead and it looks like she's going to get it."

"And since he has to drive me down, he can't port down there and back, he has to do it the old fashioned way and spend the entire day with me." Aunt Antonia looked like the famous cat who just ate the canary.

That got my gears turning. I wondered how I could convince Cody to take me car shopping? It would be fun to visit Atlanta. I was actually humming as I started the car and pulled out onto the road.

CHAPTER 18

CAN YOU DO IT

Softball. I hated playing softball, but that's what Brent loved, and it was his birthday. So everyone was in the field behind the arena playing ball.

At least his transformation had happened with no issues. He was telekinetic like her, but it was way too soon to see how strong his power would become. He was already trying out his power in minor ways. Like adjusting the flight of a ball just enough to keep it outside the swing of a bat.

Tony, his best friend had thought it was hilarious, but Paul had not seen the humor in him striking out in a softball game pitched by Lisa. Paul played on his college baseball team and had a batting average in the three hundred range.

The softball game had deteriorated into a wrestling match between the boys. The girls had used it as an excuse to end the game without hurting Brent's feelings.

Now, most of the boys were gathered around the grill getting ready to cook some burgers and the girls were laughing at their attempts. I laughed as Paul attempted to light a fire that would never start. Then he realized Lisa had formed a shield around it and the fire never reached the charcoal. At this rate, it would be tomorrow afternoon before we had dinner.

"Hungry?" Cody asked as I snuggled down into his arms and stretched my legs out toward Crystal and Mace who were in similar positions on the opposite side of the swing. Cody was nibbling on the back of my neck, making me shiver. I had my own strict rules about the amount of public displays of affection I would allow.

Crystal was a little looser about what she would let Mace get away with, but not much. Cody pulled me into a deep kiss that sent rivulets of desire along my nerve endings. I felt that kiss from the top of my head all the way to my toes. Lately, our embraces had become intense, more demanding and I know I would be facing a decision before long. Cody was going back to college in two weeks and I would be starting my senior year of high school. Long distance relationships rarely lasted. Was this one worth trying to make it work?

My mind was going to places it knew better than visiting when a startled scream ripped through the air.

Everyone forgot what they were doing and looked around to find the source.

It was Brent and he looked really scared. He had been trying to start the barbeque briquets by using his brand new TK ability. I guess he had been concentrating too hard on making fire but because it had expanded too fast and got out of hand. Most everyone had been able to avoid anything worse than a minor burn, but Brent wasn't so lucky. His skin was already red and blistered.

"Oh, Lord. He's lost control of the molecular friction and has no idea how to stop the physical reaction."

Crystal was crying, and Mace was trying to calm her down without any luck. "I can't do this again. This is what happened to Michael. Someone help him. Please."

"Memory! Where are you going?"

"I think I can help him."

"Help him. How? You can't control his powers. No one can!"

"No, but I might be able to counteract the fire long enough for him to break the cycle. It may be his only hope."

"What do you mean?" Cody looked scared. I had no idea if he was worried about Brent or me.

"I'm a lot stronger than he is. He's speeding up the elements, I'm going to slow them down."

"Do you think you can do that?"

"Hold my coke." She walked as close to the heated air as possible and began concentrating.

For a moment nothing appeared to be happening, then crystals of ice began forming in the air around her and just outside the unseen perimeter of the energized atoms. The heat from his hands melted them almost as fast as they formed. But at least he was not getting any hotter. I could see the hope forming in his eyes, but fear was written all over his face. Brent knew he was already badly burnt but at least if I could overcome the flames, he would have a chance to survive.

Gradually the ice field expanded. Inch by inch it pushed back the flames in the air around Brent. The air was no longer steaming but it was still extremely hot. Even more important, Brent seemed to be regaining some control over the swirling atoms and he was no longer pushing the atoms to move faster. In less than a minute it was over, but it felt as if it had taken a week to do it. My muscles were trembling, and I slid down onto my knees on the grass.

Brent was far from okay. He stood in the same position with his arms stretched out, afraid to move them lest the movement of the joint caused the skin to pull apart. His skin was black and cracking anywhere the clothes had not covered it. She was certain underneath the thin cotton material it was red and blistered almost as badly as the exposed skin.

"Stay still, don't move. There's got to be something I can do " Porting him out was not an option. Hugo had stressed the fact that a non-teleporter could not jump. Then I thought of a possibility. A wild idea, one that I might not be able to pull off. But it might be the only chance Brent had.

"It could work. It had to work," I muttered. "Brent! Stay as still as you can. Do not move." She sent a mental tentacle out to her friends.

Crystal, I need his parents here. Can you contact Hugo and have him bring them as fast as possible? Make sure you warn Hugo about what happened. In fact, he needs to bring Antonia here first, she's a doctor. Make sure she brings her medical bag.

I took a deep breath and tried to calm my nerves and contacted Cody.

Cody, I need your help. I need you to link with Brent and keep him calm. Don't let him panic and don't let him move.

Don't let him move! What the hell are you going to do? We need to get him to a hospital.

He can't be moved. His skin will start to fall off and the shock could kill him. Not to mention the infection he could get. The ground around him now is sterilized. It's about as clear of bacteria as possible.

So what are we going to do? Just stand here and watch him die?

*No. I hope not. Not if I can help it. *

What can you do? You can't heal him. You're not a healer.

No. But maybe I can help him heal himself.

Everyone was staring at me, wondering if I had gone crazy. I had managed to stop Brent from burning up completely, but now the initial shock was wearing off. My cousins were wondering what I was going to do next. They were scared. Hell, I was scared.

I'm going to try to get his skin to repair itself. I don't know If I can but If I can't he may die. Just link and hold him still.

Cody looked like he'd just been kicked in the stomach, but he linked up with Brent anyway.

I walked slowly around Brent studying his burns. There was very little that wasn't damaged. The fluid was starting to leak from tiny cracks in his damaged skin and that worried me. I wasn't sure what to do first. I needed someone with more experience to answer my questions.

Crystal's voice interrupted my musing and I realized Hugo and Antonia had arrived. Luckily Antonia had a strong stomach and she knew what needed to be done so Hugo left to get his parents.

Antonia didn't ask how I had stopped the re-action, she was too busy rigging up an IV to get fluids stared into his body. That took care of my first question. She needed a functional hand with a vein to stick the IV needle into.

Cody, I'm going to try to move the skin cells to the top of his hand, so Antonia can get t needle in. Try to keep him calm.

I knew I could move atoms. I tried to remember what my mother had taught me about cell regeneration. As a child, I had wondered why my logical mother had spent so much time talking about something I considered impossible at the time. But know I understood the reason. My mother had talked about how cells molecules and atoms are constantly changing. Usually, it takes two to four weeks for skin cells to reach maturity. The new cells are in the lowest level of the epidermis and it takes them about a month to make their way to the outer layer of the dermis. In the meanwhile, the aging outer layer sloughs off. Because the DNA remains the same it duplicates itself over and over again. So all I had to do is to speed up the new cell's journey to the surface so it can replace the old burnt cells. Sounded simple right?

Nope. It scared the hell out of me.

I began concentrating, trying to remember everything my mother had said. I was going to remove the dead external cells and move healthy new cells forward toward the surface. I had to do this at the molecular level. I had no idea how hard it was going to be. It took me half an hour, but both his hands were now covered in perfect skin. And I really needed to sit down again.

I turned to look for a folding chair to sit in and there she was. I recognized her instantly. The bitch who tried to kill me in the mine.

"What the hell is she doing here?" I asked. Antonia finished inserting the needle and turned to look.

During my attempt to heal Brent's hands I hadn't noticed that Hugo had returned. She was standing beside Hugo and a tall middle-aged man wearing the first pair of glasses I had seen since moving to Winters Cove. I recognized her voice, he movements, the way she stood and moved her hands. And she knew it.

"That's Brent's parents." I could tell by Antonia's eyes she already knew what I had just realized. Brent's mother had tried to kill me. For the briefest second, it crossed my mind that I could simply vanish and get my revenge on her. But Brent had never done anything to hurt me and I could not walk away from him.

His mother was scared. I think she realized I was the only chance her son had to survive. Brent was burned over eighty percent of his body. With traditional medical care, his chance of surviving, even with massive scarring one only was twenty percent. She had seen the skin on his hands regenerating. And she knew I was the one doing it.

"I will be right back."

"Memory wait…" Antonia tried to stop me, but she knew there was nothing she could say that would prevent me from doing what I intended to do.

I started walking in her direction but the closer I got to them, the harder it became. Bents mother looked just like my mother. Not similar like all the others, identical to my mother. It was surreal as well as maddening. How could I hate someone who looked so much like the woman I loved with my heart and soul?

It was clear to me that she was a very close relative of my mothers. Maybe even a sister? Just because my mom had never mentioned a sister didn't mean one didn't exist. That's when it hit me. If there was a sister, there could be more close relatives. Like a grandmother or grandfather?

Hugo followed my eyes and saw the pain reflected in them. His eyes clouded over, and he placed a hand on my arm.

Memory. Please. Think about what you are doing. Please don't risk Brent's life because of what his mother had done. You are the only one who can help him.

I didn't want to listen.

You don't know what you are asking. I snapped back. I wanted to scratch her eyes out. Run over her with a car. Open up the ground beneath her feet and let her feel the terror I had felt as the earth collapsed around me.

My inner voice kept reminding me I didn't know him that well anyway. Now that I thought about it, he hadn't said more than two, maybe three words to me since I arrived. Why should I care if he lives or dies?

"Yes, I do," Hugo replied, as he laid his hand on my shoulder. "Trust me. I will handle it. Just do what you can to save Brent. Please."

"You've got to be kidding." I jerked my arm away and teleported.

"I could hear Cody calling me, but I ignored him.

I needed a moment alone. I needed to punch the bitch in the face. No. I needed to take her into the caved in mine and leave her, let her feel how I felt being trapped inside with rocks and dirt falling around me.

I sighed. *I needed to flush the toilet and go back to help Brent.*

Cody looked relieved when I reappeared. I could tell he was worried, but he didn't want

Brent to know how worried he had been, about the possibility that I might not be coming back.

Hugo and Antonia didn't say anything, but I could tell they were relieved.

"This is harder than I thought it was going to be. I need a chair to sit in. And a coke, maybe something to eat."

Antonia had given Brent something to help with the pain, but I knew he had to be getting tired of standing in the same spot. His body was swaying slightly. Antonia now held one hand while his mother held the other. She had made her put on latex medical gloves like she was wearing to reduce the change of infection, but I knew there was no way to prevent infection. We were fighting the clock and we were losing.

I knew there were no choices about what I did next. His face was a priority, but he really needed to be able to sit down. I decided to fix that problem next.

I began to concentrate. It took less energy and time to fix the back of his legs and his bottom than his hands. The skin was thicker, and he also had a much larger bed of replacement cells to pull from. His pants had given him some protection from the heat.

Fifteen minutes later, his backside was clean, and he could sit down.

Then Antonia reminded me that he had to bend his knees to sit. And the tissue where his legs joined the body in front needed to be done. There was a decision to be made and I wanted him to make it.

Brent, I need to ask you something. I know you are tired. I was hoping to let you sit down, but if you sit now, you could have scars on your knees and at the top of your legs. What I'm doing is taking a lot of my energy. I really wanted to do your face next, because I don't know how long it's going to take. But you are also burned around your groin. It's your choice. What do you want to be done?

He didn't say a word, he simply sat down on the chair behind him.

I know it had to hurt, even with the pain killers. The skin on his knees split and started bleeding but his instructions were clear. He wanted the groin done but logic said the face first.

His mother started crying as the blood began trickling down his knees.

I glared at her. Pity was not in my vocabulary where she was concerned.

I pulled my chair right in front of him and began piecing him back together. Against my better judgment, I began repairing his groin area, figuring he would relax and make things easier for me if his family jewels were safe. The repairs were remarkably easy. His jeans and all that loose skin protected the super important parts and it was literally a case of skimming off the steamed skin and making him comfortable.

He could barely open his eyes, but he kept them locked on my face as I worked. I hadn't mentioned what I was going to do to anyone, so no one was bothering me, asking questions. This was great because I wasn't up to discussing how I saved my closest blood cousins future sex life.

When I finished, I simply winked and watched a visible wave of relief swept over his body. I suspected that if his tear ducts were not fused together, there would be tears rolling down his cheeks. Men got emotional about the damnest things.

I shook myself all over, moving as many muscles as possible without being obvious. Then I began studying his face trying to figure out the most important order of repairs.

I decided his lips were damaged the worse, so

I started there. It was amazing how many blood vessels were in a pair of lips. And how much fat. The cell level I used for repairs was only four layers down, so I was able to repair them relatively quick. Since I was working outward, I moved directly to his nose and chin. The chin wasn't difficult at all, there was not a lot of intricate details involved. And I was getting better with practice.

His nose was definitely tricky. The nostrils on both sides were burnt away and I had to stimulate the cartilage to rebuild the foundation before I could cover them with new skin. I had never tried building cartilage before. His nose was not exactly as it had been before. I hadn't really paid much attention to his face, so I used Cody's nose as a pattern.

Once I got the first layer of new skin on, I moved to the area around his eyes. I knew the most important thing to do was to take care of the essentials, there were excellent plastic surgeons if it came down to that, my job was to keep him alive.

It tore me up to see the fear in his eyes when I slumped in exhaustion before completing the cosmetic portion of the skin repair. He could open and close his eyes and they were healed enough that he could see the damage to his arms and the front of his legs. He could imagine how bad his face looked.

Antonia and Cody both grabbed for me as I fainted.

***

I awoke to find myself sprawled out on a blanket under a tree, with my head in Cody's lap. He was stroking my cheek as he talked to me; as if I was awake and listening to him the entire time.

"…could hold out as long as you did. Brent is going to live thanks to you. Antonia is pumping him full of antibiotics and pain killers. Once you have rested a while, you can finish, so stop complaining and rest."

"I feel better. How long have I been out of it?"

"About an hour. But I had to go deep and convince your subconscious that you needed to rest, or you would have burnt yourself out trying to do it all at once."

"How is he?" He still needed so many repairs.

"He's resting too. Antonia knocked him out after his mother and father got into a knock-down drag-out shouting tirade over her trying to kill you. His father kept screaming, if Brent dies, it would be your fault."

"He's right." I could see her now, sitting on the ground nearby, so she could keep her eyes on her son as he slept. I remembered all the times I wished my mother could have been there to hold me when I was upset. She obviously loved her son. What I couldn't understand was why she hated me?

"I had no idea she was involved until today. Most people would be petty, throwing Brent to the dogs out of spite. I'm glad you are not that type of person."

Except it had crossed my mind.

***

Hugo's right eyebrow raised for just a second when he overheard the two teenagers talking. He needed to have a talk with Memory when this was over and explain a few things. Things most of the family did not know. He had been sworn to secrecy years ago, but he realized now might be a good time to break a promise. It couldn't hurt and it might help Memory to understand the reasons behind the animosity.

He watched as Cody helped Memory to her feet and then support her as she walked over to where Brent was sleeping. Memory settled down beside him and went back to work, allowing him to sleep as she manipulated the molecules making up his skin, moving the dead ones away from his face as she shifted the newer, healthy ones from the layers below into position. Rebuilding the tissues of the face was exacting detailed work. She had a recent photo his father provided, that was helping her but there would always be tiny differences caused by damage to the underlying support tissue in the extremely damaged areas. It would be close, but not perfect.

No one knew he had been the one to locate Memory. It had been luck that made him hire a detective four years earlier.

He had wanted to see how fast a particular stock had risen in value during the early months after its public release. While browsing through the archives of an old San Francisco newspaper looking for information related to a stock he was interested in purchasing he'd discovered the first lead. Underneath one of the reports was a photo of Margot and her husband Billy, and the title 'Three die in Auto Accident, Child Survives.'

That had been the first hint the family had as to what had happened to Margot after she disappeared. She had changed her name, as had her husband. But there had been no question of who she was. He had loved her for most of his teenage years and his heart would have recognized her anywhere.

He blamed himself for her leaving. They had been dating for a couple of weeks when Antonia found out she was pregnant with Diana. There was no way he could turn his back on the mother of his child. They had gotten married, but it had never been a love match. Margot had changed after the news of the baby was announced. She started running with a wilder crowd and hanging out in Gatlinburg with kids from the reservation. That's where she met Memory's father. When they ran off together, it had torn him apart. Finding her daughter and bringing her home had helped, but nothing would ever take away the memories that haunted him.

Watching her work to save the life of the son of the woman who had tried to kill her, he realized how proud of her he was. Diana his daughter was living in Europe with Eka's daughter Heidi. She had left after Michael's funeral, claiming she could not handle being in the valley any longer. In time, he hoped she would return.

Since he had stepped into his position within the family, things had fallen apart one by one, until he was not certain he could handle any more. Now, this happened.

Brant, Brent's father had not said much after learning what his wife had done to Memory. Hugo had seen a defeated man before, but he could not ever remember seeing someone look as overwhelmed by circumstances as his best friend.

Brant walked around in a daze, mumbling one-word answers to any question asked when he bothered answering at all. His eyes remained locked on Memory as she struggled to repair his son's injuries, and nothing would distract him until she was finished. The fire had brought to light more than Brent's injuries. Unfortunately, Memory could not repair the damage to Brant's heart.

***

The first hints of sunlight were peaking over the eastern ridge as I sat back on my heels and stretched. Not that it helped. All the stretching in the world would not relieve the tension in my muscles. I had been pulling energy from my own body to generate the kinetic force necessary to move the cells upward.

"I think that's it. I found a spot on the sole of his foot behind his big toe I had missed earlier. I really need to get some sleep now. Do me a favor Brent, no more experimenting until you have learned some control. It took me a weeks before I tried lighting a candle."

"No problem," Brent replied," After going through that, I doubt I'll ever try to make fire again."

Memory gave him a wan smile and allowed Cody to help me to my feet. She gave him a quick kiss. " I think I'm going to get Hugo to boost me a ride back to the house, I'm too tired to try it alone. Call me in a few hours, Okay?"

"Go get some sleep. I'll drop by later this afternoon and wake you in person."

His eyebrows wiggled like a lecherous old man and she started laughing. "If I wasn't so tired, I'd slap you for that."

"Go. Antonia wants to give Brent one last check before she sends him home to bed for a few days' rest. She's making him strip and he prefers her to be the only female to see him au natural today."

I walked over to Hugo and explained my request.

He nodded and they disappeared. Hugo was gone less than a minute before he returned.

Brent was standing in his boxer briefs now, and Cody was doing a cursory search of his body to ensure Memory had not missed anything. His curly blonde locks were gone. Memory had removed the fire damaged skin on his head. Antonia was sure it would grow out again.

"Memory did a fantastic job," Antonia said to her husband. "I told him no baths or showers for twenty-four hours. And no solid foods today. That seemed to bother him more than anything. He wanted to order pizza as soon as he got home. I don't want to risk internal damage to the lining of his throat. He had scorched the inside of his mouth and throat, and she had to repair his lungs too."

"When I saw him, I expected to be attending another funeral."

"You and me both. If I had not seen her working on him, I would not have believed it was possible."

"I imagine Nedra is thinking about a few of the choices she's made too." He replied as Cody and Brent walked slowly toward Brant's silver SUV. Nedra was already sitting inside. Brant was heading their way instead of the car. He looked bad.

"We are going home. I ...I need a day to think. So much...I can't believe she..." He stopped talking and slapped Hugo on the shoulder in a brief hug.

" Later Bro. It will all work out."

As Brant shuffled toward the SUV he wondered if what he'd said was true. A lot had happened. " Let's go home."

Then he laughed and shouted, "Cody, wait up. We need a ride home.

***

I strutted through the double glass doors, grinned and waved my driver's license overhead. It was almost a month since my birthday and it was long overdue. Uncle Matt tossed me the keys and walked around to get in the passenger side of my new Infiniti Qx50. I had considered so many cars before I compromised and got the compact SUV. It seems a four wheel is a necessity in the mountains. So I could check two things off my to-do list.

Next was the party. Cody would be leaving in two days, so I was really looking forward to the celebration.

Brent was doing great, and other than a few tiny changes to his appearance, he was showing no sign of the trauma he'd experienced. We were going to celebrate our birthdays later than expected, but I could not wait. It was my very first birthday party.

Since it was a family celebration everyone would be there. Higo said no excuses. That made me smile.

"What are you looking so happy about?" Uncle Matt knew me well. He could tell I was looking forward to more than a birthday cake.

"Oh, just thinking about tonight." I kept my eyes on the road.

He looked at me for a moment and then relaxed.

It was almost five and the party was scheduled to start t seven. We had just enough time to grab a quick shower and head out for the party. Aunt Peggy and Dodi had already left. They were helping Antonia with the food and all the little details that went into a family get together.

I was practically bouncing as we pulled into the parking area at Hugo and Antonia's. I had to fight the impulse to run to find Cody and Crystal.

"Wow, you are really excited. Slow down, they won't start the party without you."

"I know. Do you think everyone is here?"

"Looks like everyone except Brant and Nedra. But I think I see their car coming now." He was looking back toward the main road.

"Okay. Well, I'm going to find Cody and Crystal. " I was whistling as I walked toward the twinkling lights set up around the pool.

Cody had saved me a chair. I slid into it and waved my driver's license around, basking in the scattered congratulations. Everyone was laughing and talking.

"What the hell?" Brent gasped.

Silence descended on the group. Crystal had to cover her mouth with her hand to keep from blurting out something random.

Cody squeezed my hand and I slowly raised my eyes to see what was so startling.

Standing just inside the lighted enclosure was Brant and Nedra. As usual, they were dressed to the nines in the latest fashion from Paris. Brant's face was flaming as he shook Hugo's hand. Nedra didn't say a word.

She was wearing a gorgeous white silk jumpsuit. It was the perfect foil to set off her blue, pink and green hair…and body.

Lisa blurted out, "She looks like a giant Easter egg!"

I didn't say a word. It hadn't been easy to port the dye tablets into her shower head. Food coloring was impossible to wash off, it had to wear away. She would be wearing those colors for a while.

I smiled.

Now it was a great day…

I hope you enjoyed the story.
Please leave a review.

V C Sanford is part of the Bell, Book & Claw
family.

Join us on Facebook
@vcsanford

or on Instagram
@vcsanfordbooks